Kilimanjaro Snow

Enjoy

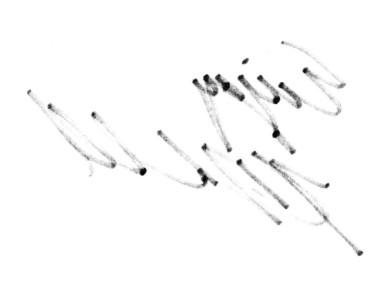

Kilimanjaro Snow

A Finn Pilar Key West Mystery

LEWIS C. HASKELL

ABSOLUTELY AMAZING eBOOKS

Published by Whiz Bang LLC, 926 Truman Avenue, Key West, Florida 33040, USA.

For information contact:
Publisher@AbsolutelyAmazingEbooks.com

ISBN-13: 978-1945772597 (Absolutely Amazing Ebooks)
ISBN-10: 194577259X

Kilimanjaro Snow

PRIMARY CHARACTERS

Thomas 'Abacus' Finch – Finn's business partner in *The Mockingbird* Bar

Ernesto Finnegan 'Finn' Pilar – Navy Seal drop out, former Key West cop, part-time insurance investigator, and bar owner

Crutch- Finn's three-legged rescue dog and his sidekick

Officer Jeff 'OJ' Sessions – Finn's former partner on the Key West Police Force and now a detective

Stacy Barnett– Finn's lawyer and love interest

Matt Divine – Former Navy Seal instructor, owner of insurance investigation firm *Divine Interventions* and Finn's employer

Henri 'Hank' Dupree – Eccentric millionaire, grandson of Irenee Dupree Jr. and developer of the 'Smokin' Hot' hemp body sports car

Edwin 'Whiner' King – Former Navy Seal and owner of *'Blunt Force'* Security

Consuelo – Henri's transgender bodyguard and housekeeper/cook

Digby 'Digger' Graves – Key West Medical Examiner

Giselle 'GG' Graves – wife of Digger Graves

Annalee – Cuban Tour guide

Nieve – Cousin of Annalee

Ricardo Ramos – Owner of *Azul Primero,* a tequila company, an investor in The Mockingbird and owner of an ocean racing super boat

Dale Baldwin – Former Marine Force Recon Operator and Owner of *Worldwide Weapons Force - WWF*

Harry Street – National Geographic Photographer and owner of Tripod

Lon and Rosie – Captain and first mate of *Kilimanjaro*

Carl Wallace – Special Operator for Blunt Force

Sylvia – Clerk at Key West Police Headquarters

CHAPTER ONE

The ragged, salt-stained sloop drifted toward shore inside the shallows behind the reef surrounding Key West. It rammed into the stern of a live-aboard anchored off Wisteria Island amidst the thirty or so others, either moored or derelict, just off shore. Many boats in this offshore fleet are anchored there to avoid paying long-term dock fees at nearby Garrison Bight or the A&B Marina.

The live-aboard owner charged up on deck to see what idiot had rammed his boat. When no one responded to his angry shouts, he hooked a line on the offending boat's damaged bowsprit and climbed aboard to see if the captain was asleep, drunk, stoned or all three. The moment he opened the hatch and stepped onto the companionway ladder, he almost vomited on the deck sole.

Tied below on a settee in the cabin was someone who at one time might have been an attractive, well-endowed young woman, now clearly dead. She wore a knife wound across her throat and not a stitch of clothing covering the rest of her. The smell indicated her death had not been recent. The owner rushed back up the companionway to the rail, puked his morning coffee and Apple Fritter over the side, then clamored back aboard his own boat and hailed the Coast Guard on Channel 16.

"Coast Guard, Coast Guard, Coast Guard. This is the sailboat *Blue Agave* declaring an emergency. Repeat, this is the sailboat *Blue Agave* declaring an emergency. Come in, please! Over."

Blue Agave, Blue Agave, Blue Agave, this is Coast Guard Station Key West, go to Channel 4 and state the nature of your emergency. Over."

"Coast Guard, Coast Guard, Coast Guard, going Channel 4. Over."

"Go ahead *Blue Agave*. Over."

"Coast Guard, this is *Blue Agave*. I'm anchored off the backside of Wisteria and was just rammed by a sailboat with no captain on board; only a dead woman with her throat slashed in the cabin. Over."

For the next two hours, Abacus Finch, the owner of *Blue Agave*, sat on his deck explaining what had happened, first to the Coast Guard, then to Key West police officers.

No, he had not seen the other boat approaching his boat. No, he did not know who owned the boat. No, he had never seen the boat before and no, he did not recognize the girl, etc., etc., etc.

As Abacus told me the story later that morning, I was intrigued. It may have been the offending boat's name, *Kilimanjaro,* which triggered my interest.

~ ~ ~

My name is Ernesto Finnegan Pilar, or as my friends call me 'Finn'. I was named Ernesto after my father's love of Hemingway and Finnegan for my mother's Irish heritage and her love of James Joyce. Any boat named *Kilimanjaro* had to have some connection to one of my personal favorite Hemingway short stories, 'The Snows of Kilimanjaro'.

Abacus and I are currently partners in a local Key West bar named the *Mockingbird* that specializes in tequila. We had been friends during our younger years working in accounting in San Diego. When I left the firm to join the Navy and become a Navy SEAL, he continued grinding it out doing audits and playing the field in the Gaslamp Quarter of San Diego.

I dropped out of BUD/S, the initial Navy Seal training due to injuries then completed my tour with Explosive Ordinance Disposal or EOD. I met a beautiful girl from Key West who I married after I finished in the Navy and we moved to her home in Key West where I began working as a cop. I was fired from the force and believe me, it's hard to have that happen in Key West but that's another story.

"Did the Coast Guard find anything on the boat?" I asked.

"You mean besides the dead body?" he replied sarcastically.

"Boy, you're in a shitty mood today. Of course besides the body," I retorted.

"Of course I'm in a shitty mood," he snapped. "What do you expect after getting a chunk of my swim platform smashed and the rudder damaged? " he replied.

"Okay, okay, let me know when you stop feeling sorry for yourself and then tell me the rest of the story."

It was hot and I had just gotten back from taking a tour of trees and newspaper boxes with *Crutch*, my three-legged rescue mutt, and closest companion. I was sweaty, tired, and a bit hung over. I needed my morning swim and a Bloody Mary so I was not in my most sympathetic frame of mind.

"Fuck you, Finn," he mumbled as he walked away.

I called after him, "Wait, wait, wait, hang on man. Did the dead girl have any ID on her?"

"What, on her naked, bloody body?" he growled. He really was in a snarky mood.

"You're right, it was a dumb question."

"No shit, Sherlock," he replied. He loved to call me Sherlock, referring to my other 'job' as a part-time insurance investigator for my old BUD/S instructor's company, *Divine Interventions*. With a name like Matt Divine, what do you expect?

"All right, enough," I said with my tail between my legs. "You have good reason to be in a shitty mood. So why did they keep you for two hours? What else did they find on the boat and were they able to identify the girl?"

"What, so now you're interested in my little problem?" he said with not a little sarcasm. "You mean a murdered girl is not enough?"

"Abacus, time out. I know it's tough. Just tell me the story again with all the details," I encouraged.

He took a deep breath, paused then began slowly. "I had just poured my second morning cup of coffee when the boat took a major lurch. I spilled the damn coffee on my best shorts and burned my thigh."

In his case, he meant his oldest shorts. No wonder he was cranky but in reality, it was not the first spill they had endured. It was usually rum or tequila that was spilled on them so the coffee might be a sobering relief for the shorts. In his mind, however, they were just broken in.

He continued. "I ran up the companionway to find what looked to be a Beneteau Oceanis 41 jammed up my fucking ass," he cursed. "Its bow was crushing my swim platform, and the bowsprit was jammed into the spokes of my wheel with its Bruce anchor hooked on my stern safety lines."

He paused to catch his breath then continued. "I yelled out but no one answered, so I tried to unhook it and push it off my stern. It was too wedged on so I tied a line on one of its bow stanchions and climbed onto the bow.

I went along the starboard side and into the cockpit then opened the hatch. The stink was overpowering but I only had to look below to see the body of the girl lying on the sofa in the cabin. Between the stink and decay, it was obvious she was dead. I left the hatch open and climbed back on board the *Blue Agave* and called the Coast Guard."

"What did they find on board other than the girl?" I asked again.

"I really don't know," he said. "They got to the Beneteau in under ten minutes, went aboard for about another ten minutes, then came onto the *Blue Agave* to take a statement from me about what I knew."

"So you saw the girl lying on the settee in the cabin salon, right?" I questioned.

"Yeah, she was on her back sort of laid out with her arms by her sides." he said with his eyes downcast.

"Could you see any scars or tattoos on her at all?" I asked.

"Come on man, it was all I could do to hold my breath long enough to keep from puking into the cabin . . . " He paused. "Wait a sec. Yea, I saw what looked like an outline of a cat sitting on a new moon tattooed above her right breast. Weird thing to have there I thought." He looked up at me and saw my face.

"Finn, what's wrong man?"

It couldn't be, I thought as the blood drained from my face and I turned pale as freshly fallen snow.

CHAPTER TWO

Not long after my divorce and getting fired from the Key West Police Department, I went on a six-month 'feeling sorry for myself ' bender. With my friend Matt's help, I was able to begin rebuilding my life and I even signed up for the Havana Challenge, a sailboat race between Key West and Havana.

This race was designed to encourage 'People-to-People' interaction as relations with Cuba began to open up. I was not a participant sailor but rather went with my buddy Lee and his yellow Labradoodle *Dijon*. We sailed on his sixty-one foot Privilege catamaran *Sea Monster* as a support boat for the racing crews.

~ ~ ~

The Strait of Florida between Key West and Havana can be a treacherous waterway. The Atlantic Ocean and the Caribbean Sea meet near Key West and it has been a graveyard for hundreds of ships going back to the 1600s. Key West was notorious for the wreckers who prowled the waters ostensibly rescuing the crews from wrecked ships off its coast. The less generous in the press hinted that the locals placed lights in safe areas directing ships to steer toward the reefs with the intention of claiming the cargos for salvage.

My ex father-in-law's family got their start as wreckers in the Strait and the devious trade at one time helped Key West become the richest per capita city in the U.S. I only discovered the family's Machiavellian tendencies after my failed marriage to his daughter and being kicked off the KWPD. Clearly, I'm not over it but I digress.

~ ~ ~

The race between Key West and Havana is followed by three days in Havana involving a 'cultural exchange'; read drinking *Havana Club* rum at various haunts in and around the city each claiming some relationship with Hemingway. In Cuba, Hemingway is an almost mythic figure, a bit like Jimmy Hoffa in the U.S. Papa seemed to have been a regular at almost every bar, hotel and marina in the Havana.

One afternoon we were drinking *Cristal,* a popular local beer at Hotel Ambro Mundos in Old Havana when our tour guide came into the bar. Annalee was a beautiful girl with long black hair and a quirky dimpled smile who had been showing us the sights of Havana.

"Are you boys up for a little fishing this evening?" she asked with her sweet Cuban accent. "The local boys go out each evening on, how you say, their floats, to fish. My brother goes out and offered to take you and teach you how to fish *Cuban style.*"

After having finished three beers each, Lee and I agreed that would be a great idea although not having a clue what she was talking about.

"If you can be at the Castropole Restaurant on the Malecon at six o'clock, you can meet my brother Jorge. He usually goes with my uncle Raul but Raul is visiting my parents in Holguin. They run a Casa Particular there."

I couldn't resist asking, "What's a Casa Particular?"

"In Cuba," she began, "Many people open their homes to tourists as a way to earn extra money. The government licenses them and takes a percentage. It is a very inexpensive way to visit Cuba."

Wanting to sound modern I replied, "Sounds like a Cuban Airbnb."

She smiled, "Yes we think we invented it. You can now even make reservations online just like Airbnb."

I was beginning to think Cubans were a lot more entrepreneurial than most of us in America.

We agreed to meet up at six and I went back to my hotel for a change of clothes and my bathing suit. I had an hour to kill before going down to the Malecon so I hopped in a Coconut Taxi for a quick run up to Hotel Nacional.

Hotel Nacional is a famous hotel on the Malecon, a nine-kilometer long concrete wall, and promenade that runs along the harbor in Old Town Havana. The hotel was notorious as a favorite haunt of American Mafia types in the forties and fifties. It was also on a point where troops and antiaircraft guns were located in trenches during the Cuban Missile crisis in the early sixties after the Cuban Revolution. Today it is *the* high-end place to stay in Havana.

After a tour of the hotel defences plus a couple of Cuba Libres, I headed down to the Castrople Restaurant to meet Annalee and Jorge. Lee begged off saying he wanted to check on his boat at the marina but I suspected a little traveler's revenge might be the real reason.

As I arrived, Annalee was standing on the Malecon opposite the restaurant with a young guy I assumed was her brother. Next to him was what appeared to be a six foot by six foot Styrofoam float about eighteen inches thick and wrapped in a cage of narrow wooden strips. He had a bamboo fishing-pole in his hand, his arm around Annalee's shoulder and a smile on his face.

"Hola, señor Finn," he said waving the pole at me.

I tentatively waved back and replied, "Hola.

Jorge?" I inquired with my best Spanish pronunciation.

"Si," he said widening his smile.

Annalee jumped in and said, "Finn, this is my brother. His English is a bit limited but he is going to take you out on his float."

"We are going out on that?" I asked skeptically.

"Si, Si, Señor Finn. Very good boat," he said as he patted it proudly. "Catch much good fish on it."

I must have looked doubtful for Annalee said, "Jorge is one of the best fishermen in the harbor. He has been able to catch as many as ten fish a night."

The thought of spending a night floating on a queen size Styrofoam mattress in the Caleta de San Lazaro with a teenager who spoke little English was not on my top ten things to do in Havana, even with Annalee on board.

Somehow I had pictured Hemingway's boat the *Pilar*, a bottle of Havana Club Reserva and the lovely Annalee followed by a quiet late dinner at Castropol, then dancing, then . . .

"Sounds great," I heard myself say with as much enthusiasm as I could muster.

"You boys have fun. Finn I will see you bright and early in the morning," she said.

"Hang on, you're not going?" I asked, the disappointment apparent in my voice.

"No of course not. The boat is only able to support two people." This was not the *People to People* interaction for which I had anticipated or hoped.

With the theme song from Gilligan's Island playing in my head, Jorge and I lifted what I began to think of as the *Minnow* over the sea wall and into the bay.

"Just sit right back,
And you'll hear a tale.

A tale of a fateful trip,
That started from this tropic port,
Aboard this tiny ship."

I must have been humming the song louder than I thought because Jorge laughed and said, "Si, Si Señor Finn, Gilligan."

Jorge climbed off the sea wall and the rocks at its base then slipped on his swim fins and jumped off the mattress. He guided us out into the harbor about five hundred yards, propelled by his swim fins pushing from behind the *Minnow*. I knelt on the raft trying not to fall into the murky water. Apparently, he knew some special fishing hole. He had a big grin on his face and seemed to be immensely enjoying his efforts or maybe it was my discomfort.

After what seemed like an eternity but really only about twenty minutes of paddling, we seemed to settle on the best spot and he threw a small anchor over the side.

"Señor, Finn, you sit there." He pointed, asking me to sit on one side of the boat while he knelt on the opposite side with his pole. I suddenly began to suspect that my presence was purely to counterbalance his weight on the tippy little foam 'mattress'.

After about ten minutes, the tip of the pole dipped and he jerked it up. I almost lost my balance and fell in. "Joder!" Jorge seemed to curse, as the fish he was trying to snag scooted away. I didn't know what it meant but it was probably not 'darn'. He turned to me and said apologetically, "Disculpe."

Again he waited patiently and again the pole dipped, he jerked, then again "Joder!" but no disculpe this time.

Again he waited patiently then the pole tip dipped, and he jerked up. The third time was the charm and he came up with a fifteen-inch long grouper. Jorge grinned and said, "Muy bien, eh Señor Finn?"

I was impressed and replied, "Si, muy bien."

This activity continued for the next two hours with a lot of 'joders' and the occasional grin. In the end, we caught four fish and I only fell one time into the polluted soup that is the harbor. Around nine thirty, the waves and wind picked up and we headed in toward the base of the Malecon. As we approached the rocks at the base of the seawall, it was clear that we were in for a beating. It reminded me of the exit from the ocean beneath the Hotel Del Coronado during the first phase of Navy Seal training in BUD/S.

As one of the really risky evolutions during BUD/S, boat crews of eight guys each had to time the approach to the rocky landing on the beach just right, control the Combat Rubber Raiding Craft (CRRC), get out of it and drag it ashore without breaking anything in the process. It was one of the most dangerous evolutions in training and we lost several guys in my class to broken legs, ankles, and blown knees twisted on the rocks.

As I came back into focus after the flashback, I could see that Jorge was looking a little worried.

"Jorge," I began. "No problema," I said in my best Spanish and smiled.

As I began to get a feel for the wave intervals, my training came back to me even after more than a decade. We needed to catch a wave as early as possible and ride it into just before it hit the rocks then slide off the back and paddle like hell before the next one came in. We had only an eight-second interval between waves to get us both up on the rocks. Then we could bring the boat up on the next wave. Jorge seemed to be counting like I was so this was clearly not his first rodeo.

I needed to let him know I understood. As the next

wave rolled beneath us, I yelled, "Uno, dos, tres, cuatro, cinco, seis, siete, ocho, si?" Jorge was a sharp kid and got it that I understood. He nodded, "Si." He got on one side of the *Minnow* and I got on the other.

As the next wave rolled under us, we both jumped into the water and swam like hell. Our timing was a bit off but as the wave broke, we scrambled up on the slippery algae-covered rocks just in time for the boat to come crashing on us with the following wave.

Suddenly Jorge slipped and dropped back into the dark water as the float began crashing down again on top of him. In BUD/S, someone would have broken a leg or crushed a vertebra with the bulky CRRC boats so I began to appreciate the fact that this was made of Styrofoam. I reached down as the float caught the next wave and started to slam into him. I grabbed the collar of his shirt and hauled him up sputtering and coughing before the float hit the rocks.

"Gracias Señor Finn, you save me," he said.

"No," I insisted, "you would have been fine. Maybe a bump on the head," as I hit the side of my head to help him understand but he kept saying, "You save me! You save me!"

He caught his breath, gave the universal thumbs-up sign and together we lifted the float over the wall.

After catching my breath I asked. "Cerveza?"

"Si, muchas cervezas," he smiled.

We both laughed and loaded his float on a two-wheeled dolly he used to bring it to the harbor and we headed over to the Castropol for beer and fish tacos.

"Yo invito Señor Finn for save me," as he pulled out some soggy Cuban pesos to show it was his treat.

It turned out he was a student at the local university studying medicine and hoping to someday go to the U.S. He fishes as a way to supplement his income and help his parents make ends meet. Their

Casa Particular, called the *Cat on the Moon*, is successful by Holguin standards but Holguin is not a tourist center like Varadero.

We finished our Cristals and I thanked him for taking me fishing. Exhausted I returned to my hotel and crashed for the night.

~ ~ ~

The next day I met up with Lee and Annalee for breakfast in the hotel dining room. You would think I was some combination of a real-life Dirk Pitt and Superman.

"Señor Finn," Annalee gushed, "My brother told me about what happened last night. Our family and I would like to thank you from the bottom of our hearts for saving Jorge's life. If there is ever anything we can do for you, please feel free to call us."

Lee was looking at me as if to say, 'What the hell is this all about?'

I realized that nothing I could say would change her mind so I decided to be gracious. "Anyone would have done the same thing, Annalee. Please tell your brother that he is an extraordinary fisherman and I would be honored to go fishing with him anytime." *With that, I might have been telling a teeny white lie.*

After breakfast, Lee and I returned to his sailboat moored at the Marina Hemingway for our trip back to Key West. As we prepared to cast off, Annalee came up and gave me a less than chaste kiss, practically burying her tongue down my throat. I almost jumped off the boat and back on the dock. She handed me a card and invited me to return anytime.

Perhaps things might have been different if I had.

CHAPTER THREE

I told Abacus that I needed to get back to the house to check something then raced back to my small cottage. I was lucky enough to have purchased a typical shotgun cottage a couple of years ago with the help of my old BUD/S instructor Matt Divine after my divorce. I quickly began rummaging in my office desk drawers for the card that Annalee had given me years before when I left Cuba. I'd never found the time to return but I remembered with a certain lusty enthusiasm *the kiss* on the docks of Marina Hemingway. Damn, I hoped it wasn't her who lay dead in the salon of *Kilimanjaro*.

After flipping through several stacks of business cards, I once again made a mental note that I needed to set up a better card filing system. I finally found the card for Annalee and quickly placed a call. After several rings, a message said, "Has alcanzado Annalee. No estoy aquí ahora mismo así por favor dejar un mensaje y devolveré su llamada."

Not speaking Spanish, I assumed this was the usual, "You have reached Annalee.... " so I left a message. "Annalee, this is Finn Pilar. I'm not sure you remember me but we met several years ago during the Key West to Havana sailboat race. Something has come up and I need to talk to you as soon as possible."

Given the size of my ego I figured she probably remembered my name but on the off chance that the kiss was more meaningful to me than to her, I figured I had better remind her. I left my cell number and with Crutch in tow, we hopped on my scooter and headed over to the police dock off the Truman Waterfront where Abacus said they had taken the *Kilimanjaro*.

The *Kilimanjaro* was moored at the end of a floating finger dock and looked a bit forlorn surrounded by yellow police caution tape and several detectives in HazMat suits walking on deck.

I walked up the dock toward the boat and was stopped by a uniformed KWPD cop.

"Can I help you, sir?" he asked with a voice an octave or so above normal. Nerves of steel these newer beat cops. I figured he was new as he didn't recognize me.

"Finn Pilar, officer. I am from Divine Intervention Insurance Investigations." I offered. "I have been hired by the owner of the boat that was hit by this vessel."

A voice in one of the HazMat suits called out, "Don't believe any of the bullshit he tells you, Rogers."

I smiled. Yes, it was sort of bullshit but I didn't need my old partner 'OJ' Sessions giving me away.

"OJ, my man, what're you doing here?" I asked. "Last time I heard, you were on nipple patrol for Fantasy Fest. What, now you're on suspicious deaths or death by misadventure?"

"It may surprise you, Finn, but my extraordinary investigative talents and heroic behavior during your last little adventure were recognized by the Chief and I was promoted to Detective 1st Class," he replied with not a little smug pride.

With barely contained mirth, I replied, "Great you can buy the next round at the Mockingbird given your newfound status and commensurate pay increase. Until then, I may be able to help you become the Chief!" I offered.

"And how, pray tell, might you do that?" he asked skeptically.

"First I need to see the body and the crime scene."

"Screw you, Finn. Besides, she is already at the morgue and this case looks like a pretty simple case of drug smuggling gone bad. She was probably just arm-candy to keep the smugglers warm during the trip, then became a loose end once they offloaded the coke."

"Jesus, OJ, I really did underestimate you. You figured all that out before you even have the Medical Examiner's report?" I questioned sarcastically.

"Fuck you, Finn. It's called a *working hypothesis*."

I was starting to get pissed and said, "Is that 1st class detective speak for, 'develop a theory and search for evidence to support the theory'?"

"Piss off, Finn," he said angrily, dismissing me and turning back to his examination of the cabin on the boat.

In the absence of a pithy rejoinder, I let Crutch have a pee then loaded him back on the scooter. We headed over to the morgue doing my best to spin some gravel back in OJ's direction and failing miserably. 49cc Yamaha scooters have very little torque.

Before I spoke to Annalee's family, I needed to confirm that the body on the sailboat was not hers and that the tattoo was not the Cat on the Moon I recognized. The ME is an old buddy of mine, Digby Graves and he's a regular at the Mockingbird. I called him.

"Digger."

"Yo, Finn my man, wha's up?" he asked.

For some reason, his language regresses into his earlier life as a street punk whenever I call. He had been a gang member in Chicago in his early teens when he got picked up on a sweep at a crack house on the south side. For some unknown reason, the judge gave him a

17

choice: an eighteen month holiday in juvie or enlistment in the Navy.

We met when I took some shrapnel from an IED while I was diffusing its twin about fifty yards away during my visit to beautiful downtown Fallujah. He was a Corpsman when we met and he stitched me up. During my stay at the field hospital, he came to appreciate my dumb gravedigger jokes.

Why do gravediggers laugh three times when they hear a joke? . . Once when it is told, once when it is explained to them, and once when they understand it.

I've been standing in a graveyard for three hours, and the gravedigger keeps walking past me carrying the same coffin. I think he's lost the plot.

And then there's the really old groaner about Mozart. *He was found in the dug up grave with a musical score that he was decomposing.*

Over the years we stayed in touch and about six months ago he showed up at my doorstep.

"Yo Finn, my man." he began, "Key West is scouting for a new ME and I been invited to apply. I think they want a token black doc on staff. What you think?"

We went to the Bird and after three or four or five tequila shooters, I told him he was crazy. Later that night he met Giselle, a stunning six-foot Russian transvestite fishing boat captain with crystal clear eyes and pure white, spiked hair. The rest was history. He took the job and they have been together ever since.

"I'd like to drop by and ask a few questions, Digger." Digby 'Digger' Graves got his name for obvious reasons.

"Finn, if this is about the body Abacus found this morning on the boat, OJ already called me and told me not to let you see her."

"Come on Digger, I just need to check her for

identifying marks or tattoos. I may know her."

"Finn, I know you are a player and it wouldn't surprise me if you know every girl on the island and all their tattoos but OJ is trying to keep this one quiet."

"Digger, I pleaded, "I promise I will share anything I know with OJ. Besides, you owe me one."

"Don't pull that 'owe me one' bullshit Finn. You were only in the bar when GG came in. It's not like you set us up on a blind date or anything." Digger and Giselle got married two months after gay marriage was legalized and she has gone by GG ever since.

"All right, all right. Here's the deal. The family of a woman I knew in Cuba had a Casa Particular called *Cat on the Moon*."

"Abacus said the girl he found had a tattoo above her right breast that looked like a cat sitting on a crescent moon." I paused for a second. "I called her cell phone and she didn't answer. Before I talk to her family, I want to confirm that the girl on the boat is not her. I need your help to connect the dots."

Digger sat quietly for several seconds, then said quietly, "Come down the morgue and I will let you see the body."

"Thanks, man, we're even."

I was hanging up when he said, "Finn, have you heard about the karate champion who got a SEAL Contract?" "No?" I said.

"Well, I have. The first time he saluted in BUD/S, he nearly killed himself!" Digger chuckled and hung up.

We have got to get passed these grade school jokes.

~ ~ ~

I put on Crutch's leash and together we hopped on my scooter and headed over to the morgue at the hospital on Stock Island. Stock Island is just across the Cow Key Bridge north of Key West. The Lower Keys

Medical Center is the closest thing we have to a hospital and while not a trauma center, does a decent job for most situations. They can stabilize patients for a medevac air ambulance and have you to a Miami Level 1 Trauma Center in forty-five minutes.

I met Digger in the medical center's lobby and he escorted me through a maze of corridors to the morgue. He reached for the locker containing the body of the girl from the boat then paused to look at me.

The thought of the beautiful Annalee laid cold on the slab of a locker in the Key West morgue caused me to experience a chill that began in my chest and descended to my feet. It was like opening the door to a frigid blast off the mountains in Afghanistan in winter.

I nodded to Digger who then pulled the drawer out and unzipped the body bag at the head.

The relief I felt was as intense as the wave of anxiety that had preceded it. The girl while beautiful was not Annalee although there seemed to be a slight resemblance.

As Digger continued to unzip the bag, a tattoo on her upper right breast was revealed and the winter chill returned. At this rate, I was going to develop pneumonia from the changing body temperatures. The tattoo was the familiar image of a cat with its tail hanging down sitting on the lower section of a crescent moon.

"Shit," I muttered.

"Do you know her?" Digger asked.

"No, I don't recognize her but I know the tattoo. I knew a girl in Cuba several years ago and her parents owned a Casa Particular named *Cat on the Moon*. I tried to call her today and got no answer so I was concerned it might be her."

Digger zipped up the body bag and closed the cooler.

"Any idea what this is about?" he asked as we walked out of the cool morgue and toward the hospital lobby.

"Not a clue but I have a feeling I'm going to be knee deep in it shortly."

"Okay, I'll get the tox screen back in about three days and if you think it will help, I will get it to you," Digger offered.

Damn, what was I thinking?

"Digger, thanks, again. I owe you one. Give my love to GG and the next time Stacy is in town, let's do dinner at Town and Tavern, on me."

"Make it sooner rather than later." He gave me a bear hug as I rejoined Crutch and we were off to Hog Fish Grill for a bowl of Bahamian Conch Chowder, a Bloody Mary for me and a Bud Light for him. I needed to hit the pause button.

~ ~ ~

Crutch and I were headed down North Roosevelt and back home when my cell rang. I pulled over in the Home Depot parking lot as I answered the phone. Crutch hopped off to drain some Bud.

"Hola mi amigo Finn." purred a sultry voice. "Que pasa?" It was Annalee.

"Annalee, buenas tardes. It has been a long time," I said trying to figure out how I was going to approach this conversation.

"Finn, my old friend, you called and frankly your message sounded a bit distressed. What is going on?"

Clearly my cool and collected personality had not disguised my concern on my last call to her. "Well, it's been awhile since we talked." Where to begin I thought; maybe I'll open with a bit of trivia. "Well about a year ago I got involved with an old buddy of mine working on insurance investigations."

"Awhile, AWHILE! You call three years AWHILE!"

she exclaimed rattling my inner ear.

Damn some chicks are hot tempered. It's not like we were engaged; it was only one kiss although, it was a spectacular one to be sure.

"Annalee, please let me finish," I pleaded. Okay, so I am not above a little groveling.

"Screw you, Finn," and she hung up.

I know. I have that effect on people, but I needed to talk to her. I called her back right away wondering what this was going to do to my cell phone bill.

"What?"

"Annalee, before you hang up let me explain."

"You've got thirty seconds," she spat out.

"All right, today in Key West, a sailboat drifted in and hit a friend's boat."

"Twenty seconds," she counted down.

"On board was a young woman who was dead."

"Fifteen."

"She was naked with only a tattoo on her right breast."

"You are a pervert Finn, five seconds, tick tock."

"It looked like a Cat on the Moon."

Silence.

"Annalee?" I whispered.

"Oh my god, Nieve," she sobbed.

"Annalee, who is Nieve?" Between sobs, the story came out.

"Nieve is my cousin who we adopted when she was ten. My aunt and uncle were killed in a car accident. My aunt was my mother's sister. Nieve became a sister to me," she sobbed.

"Annalee, we can't be sure it's her yet. Can you describe her to me?"

"She is beautiful, five foot ten with long dark hair and she had the Cat on the Moon tattoo done a couple of years ago to match mine, above her right breast."

"Oh God, how am I going to tell my parents?" she sobbed again.

"Before you do that, can you email me her picture and her personal details: last name, date of birth and eye color. I will check to see if it is her and get back to you later today," I said in my most sensitive voice.

"Of course, but what was she doing in Key West?" she asked.

"I was going to ask you the same thing."

"She was supposed to be crewing on a sailboat this week doing a cruise from Puerto de Vita to Varadero."

"Do you know the name of the boat and its owner?"

"No, she told me but I don't remember. A friend of hers owns a crew agency that provides crew to boats that don't know Cuban waters. The boat had some African name I think."

"Can you track down the friend?" I queried.

"It was a friend from university but I can try."

I figured I had pushed about as hard as I could to confirm that it was Nieve so I suggested, "Don't draw any conclusions until we can confirm things. You can send me her information then try to track down the friend. In the meantime don't mention anything to your family."

"Okay," she agreed.

"Annalee, don't give up hope and I will try to see if I can sort things out at this end."

"Thanks, Finn. Sorry about my earlier meltdown. I understand now you are trying to help."

We disconnected and I called OJ.

CHAPTER FOUR

"What?" he answered impatiently.

"You seem really busy. I'll just call you back later to tell you the dead girl's identity," I offered and hung up. There are times when I can be a rude asshole.

He waited five minutes then called back. "Fuck you, Finn, what have you got?"

"Well you know me, as a good citizen I hate to interrupt Key West's finest when they are busy fighting crime and such. Drunk tourists and Russian money laundering tee shirt shops clearly take priority over some naked girl found with her throat slit on a boat off Wisteria," I suggested sarcastically.

"Okay have you busted my balls enough now or do you feel the need for round two?" he asked.

"No consider yourself emasculated. Here's what I know."

I gave OJ the background including my connection with Annalee, *Cat on the Moon* and the name of the girl I suspected was the victim. Then I asked him, "What I need from you is access to the boat and your help expediting the tox screen of the girl. Can you do that?"

"Finn, I'll arrange it but you need to share what you get from the girl in Cuba and any information on the boat."

We agreed to meet at Martin's for Happy Hour at five-thirty as long as I was buying. Martin's is our favorite Happy Hour spot on the island. Half price martinis and appetizers until six can't be beat.

~ ~ ~

Until I heard from OJ on access to the boat and Annalee for a picture and info on her cousin, I was stuck so I decided to take Crutch for his mid-afternoon constitutional. We walked along Duval over to South Beach then back past Southernmost Point. This landmark usually has a chaotic gaggle of tourists lined up to get pictures taken at the giant red, yellow and black buoy that marks the southernmost publically accessible spot in the U.S.

Some argue that the White Street pier is the real southernmost point of the U.S. but nobody wants to move the ten-foot high buoy. Others insist that a point on the Naval Air Station at Truman Annex is really the southernmost point but it's not accessible to the public.

Crutch and I stopped by the buoy while he performed his usual routine of cute doggy tricks. I had adopted Crutch from the Key West Shelter about two years ago. It was around the time my old BUD/S instructor smacked me out of my self-indulgent six-month pity party rum binge after being fired from the KWPD and divorced in a messy public display.

Matt Divine, for whom I now do contract insurance investigations, had seen many a veteran in need of help and understood a dog is great source of support. During part of his stint on the SEAL teams, he had been a combat dog handler. His dog Dum-Dum, like the bullet, not the idiot, served with him on two tours in Afghanistan and was killed by an IED toward the end of their tour.

These warrior dogs are some of the best-trained and most courageous animals on the planet. They go where the SEALS go from jumping out of aircraft into combat zones to leading foot patrols searching for

IEDs. While having only three legs, Crutch is not a war dog but he knows a few.

Matt helped me train Crutch so now he does a few tricks for treats and free beer. It also gave me something to shake me out of my depression. He does the usual roll over, speaks, does a five high and five low. Then he walks on his hind legs, does a pirouette, then salutes with his one front paw.

As a three-legged dog, it's his backflip that's the hit of the show. It usually gets him a round of applause and it relieves the boredom for those waiting in line. I have begun teaching him a new trick after I opened the *Mockingbird* and no, it's not doing tequila shooters.

We continued up Whitehead then headed over to the *Mockingbird* or the *Bird* as it was called by the locals. The *Mockingbird* was the brainchild of my longtime friend Abacus Finch. We started it together about six months ago and it has become a bit of a sensation after our First Annual Key West Porn Idol event, but that is another story.

The bar specializes in Tequila and is famous for the *Tequila Firebomb*. While it's a little early in the day for one of those, I did order a Stella for me and a Bud Light for Crutch. We all have to hydrate in the tropic heat of Key West.

As we sat together in the window overlooking Duval Street, I took this quiet time to reflect on my call with Annalee.

Was the girl on the boat Annalee's cousin Nieve? If not, what was with the tattoo? How did she end up on that sailboat and how did it end up in Key West? Whose boat was it? Why was she killed?

I nudged Crutch who was already asleep with his beer only half finished. "Time to go, dude, I need to take you home so I can meet with OJ."

Crutch opened one eye, farted like only a male dog

can do and rolled over facing away from me.

"No more beer for you dude," I said to him, then called over to Abacus, "Keep an eye on Crutch for me will you, but no more beer."

He waved as I left the *Bird* for the short walk to Martin's.

OJ was already at the bar so I slipped onto a stool beside him. He waved to Luca the bartender and ordered two of whatever he was already having. He usually has the Key West Sunset Martini which was fine with me.

While we waited for the drinks, OJ gave me a quick update.

"You can go over to the boat tomorrow. It's at the Old Island Boatyard on Stock. They're pulling the boat as we speak and I told them to expect you. " I thanked him, knowing this was a big deal for him to do.

"Don't thank me yet. We've gone over the boat from stem to stern and whoever did this did a decent job of cleaning up. The only thing we found that seemed strange was two additional blood splatter samples that don't match the girl's blood type. It could be nothing, but it could be that others were on board who were also killed."

"So how the hell did it 'drift' into Key West?" I asked.

"We are interviewing all the boat people we can find to see if anyone saw it come in. Also, we are looking at webcam footage from the Weston on Sunset Key and Ocean Reef to see if anything shows up."

"My bet is somebody brought it up the channel, pointed it toward the moorings off Wisteria and went for a swim."

Luca brought over the perfect yellow and red martinis and we continued to speculate.

"So whoever did this is probably long gone," I said.

"Yeah, the problem is we have no motive. The usual would be drugs or maybe human trafficking."

We ordered several appetizers and another Sunset. They do a great Black Forest Salad and the Lamb Chop Tapas are sensational.

"Any luck yet on the tox screen?" I asked.

"No, I talked to Digger and it's being rushed but it will still take at least twenty-four hours. How about you and the girl in Cuba?" he queried.

"Let me check my email". I took out my phone and checked the emails. Two caught my attention immediately. The first was from Annalee. She had an attachment with a picture of her cousin. I looked at OJ and handed him the phone.

"Shit," he exclaimed, "I'm sorry Finn, but it sure looks like the dead girl."

I nodded in agreement.

It was a family photo with the smiling faces of Annalee and Nieve at a party with other family and friends. Nieve looked like a young Natalie Wood. She had a beautiful smile that lit up her face, long raven hair, full lips and a twinkle in her eye. She and Annalee could have been real sisters.

It was clear that the girl we found on the boat was Nieve. I was not looking forward to my call to Annalee.

"Do you want to make the call or should I?" asked OJ.

"No, but thanks for the offer. I should do it."

He looked relieved and pushed around some crumbs on his plate.

I had lost my appetite so I pushed away my food, slammed down the rest of my martini and paid the bill.

I told OJ I would call him tomorrow and then rushed out of the restaurant. It was not only the email from Annalee that triggered my haste but also the second email from an old friend on the island.

~ ~ ~

"Finn, I need your help. I think I may have killed someone." That distinctive voice had me remembering back.

Henri 'Captain Cannabis' Dupree was an eccentric multi-millionaire who was the illegitimate son of one of the ne'er-do-well heirs of Irénée Dupree. He was born in Cuba at the family castle in Varadero, known as La Mansion Xanadu. The family home had been named after the Samuel Taylor Coleridge poem *Kubla Khan*, not the disco movie with Olivia Newton-John.

In Xanadu did Kubla Khan
A stately pleasure-dome decree:
Where Alph, the sacred river, ran
Through caverns measureless to man
Down to a sunless sea.
So twice five miles of fertile ground
With walls and towers were girdled round:
And here were gardens bright with sinuous rills,
Where blossomed many an incense-bearing tree;
And here were forests ancient as the hills,
Enfolding sunny spots of greenery.

Henri was always a contrarian who rejected the Dupree family chemical fortune and spent his later years researching non-oil based products made from hemp, from fabrics and paper to biofuels, hence the nickname 'Captain Cannabis'. We just called him Hank.

He was best known in Key West as the guy who designed and built a bright red sports car with the body made from hemp fiber. He and I had met when I was on the KWPD and I had to speak to him at his mansion on Shark Key after neighbors complained about him building a car in his garage.

I fell in love with the design of his hemp car, which

to hear him explain, was designed to reflect the voluptuous female form: soft rounded front fenders and a wide shapely rear end. You could just imagine him channeling Sophia Loren or Gina Lollobrigida from fifties fame as he shaped and caressed the molds to form the body panels.

He had moved his operation to a small garage on Stock Island and he would regularly update me over martinis on various ideas he had to save the planet. The last time I had talked to him was about six months ago when he was raving about a biofuel that would make his car, not just carbon neutral, but carbon negative.

I called his cell and got voice mail, "You've reached Captain Cannabis. If you get this message I'm busy saving the planet and will get back to you when it's done; better to send me a text."

I hung up and sent a text, "Call me when you can Captain."

He called me back immediately and began to rant. "Finn, I-I-I'm in deep shit dude. I'm so fucked. You've got to help me, man. You got to help me, I'm dead, screwed and in deep shit, I'm so fucked . . ."

And on and on he went. When he finally took a breath I yelled, "Henri!" I never call him Henri.

"Henri you're repeating yourself and making no sense. Slow down and tell me what happened."

He paused. "Okay, Okay." He took a deep breath and continued. "I found out today that a girl was found dead on a boat. That boat ran into the back of Abacus' boat off Wisteria."

"Yeah, so?" I interjected.

"The boat was mine Finn. Well not really mine, but I had chartered it."

"Jesus, Hank back up, what the hell's going on?"

"Okay, You remember when I told you about the house my family owned in Cuba that was taken over by

Castro in the revolution?"

It vaguely rang a bell but after two martinis my memory degrades. Wanting to sound smart I said, "Yeah, who doesn't?"

"Well, when I was a young kid, I stayed with my grandfather before he broke his leg and left Cuba. He gave me a tour of the house he had built. He called it Xanadu and it was at the time the largest private home in Latin American. He, being a very private and suspicious man, had built a number of secret passages and rooms throughout the house. "

"Dude, get to the point," I encouraged.

" I am, I am," he shot back.

"During the tour, he took me to the basement and showed me a secret room that he used as an office. It was hidden behind the huge pipe organ. To open the secret door you needed to pull certain stops on the organ. Are you with me?" he asked.

"So far, yes," I replied.

"Last year when my father died, I inherited a bunch of boxes of old papers that I've been reviewing. In one of the files, I found a reference to a Moleskin notebook that my grandfather kept. In it, he told my father that he had outlined a formula for a hemp-based biofuel that would eventually eliminate the need for petroleum-based fuels."

"Ok-ayyy?" I replied, thinking this sounded similar to other fantasies like a perpetual motion machine or cold fusion.

"Man, I'm serious. My grandfather was a genius and he felt guilty for fucking up the world with all the oil-based products he invented."

"Got it," I replied both sheepishly and skeptically.

"With Cuba closed to Americans, my father was never able to go back but also had no idea where the notebook might be located in the house. With Cuba opening up this year, I went over last month on a People-to-People visa. Long story short, I found the notebook in the secret room at Xanadu."

"Captain, I get the family history but I'm still lost about what this has to do with the dead girl."

"I'm getting there," he said. "While in Cuba, I got the feeling I was being followed. I know what you are thinking. 'I'm being a bit paranoid' but you're not the heir to a huge fortune. My family has never really accepted me given that I'm the result of one of my father's many indiscretions."

I had to give him that one. There was no fortune in my past, except for my ex-wife's family and that only brought trouble.

"I didn't want to bring the notebook back here myself for fear that it might be confiscated so I chartered a sailboat and hired a crew to bring it back."

"Oh, shit."

"Yeah, oh shit is right. The boat was the *Kilimanjaro*."

CHAPTER FIVE

" Jesus, Hank, this is fucking nuts!"
"Well I thought I was being smart," he began speaking more slowly. "I took an overnight tourist bus about seven hundred kilometers from Havana to Holguin, then caught a cab to Puerto de Vita on the north coast. It's a tiny marina but one of the few international entry points for boats sailing in Cuban waters.

I had to smile, as I was probably one of the few people who had a clue what he was talking about.

"I chartered the boat out of the Bahamas and met it at the immigration dock in Puerto de Vita. The Frontera, that's the Cuban border patrol, went on board when it arrived with both drug and bomb sniffing dogs as part of a very thorough inspection. My bags were somewhat casually inspected then we set sail for Varadero but after I hid the notebook on the boat. The Captain and a first mate had hired a girl from Holguin to act as a translator on the trip along the north coast."

"What was her name?" I asked with trepidation.
"Nieve."
"Damn, it is just too small a world." Then I remembered that Annalee had said her father had been the Harbor Master at Puerto de Vita for many years."
"We had an uneventful trip along the north coast

as long as we checked in by radio every time we crossed between provinces."

"Once we arrived in Varadero, I taxied to Havana and flew back to Key West. The boat was to come to Key West with the notebook but something must have happened along the way."

"Thank you, Captain Obvious," I dripped sarcasm, one of my more positive traits.

"Fuck you, Finn, this is serious."

"All right, I get it, but who would want to steal this notebook and how would they even know about it?"

"Every oil company in the world would like to steal it but my bet is that the family firm, Dupree Petroleum, is the prime candidate. I would bet the family knew about the file in the papers they sent me but couldn't locate the Moleskin notebook referred to in the file."

"It's all speculation, but perhaps they hoped I might know something so they sent the papers to me. Dupree Petroleum then had me followed when I went to Cuba to retrieve the notebook at Xanadu and were looking for an opportunity to steal it."

I reflected on this theory and in the absence of anything better agreed that it was as good a start as any.

"But why kill Nieve and what about the rest of the crew? And how did they take over the boat?"

Hank thought for a moment then shrugged, "I have no idea, but if this formula is real it could mean billions for the company who can patent it."

I thought for a minute. DP is the family oil company and they are on the ropes with all the lawsuits after the oil spill on their drilling rig *Deep Ocean* last year in the Gulf. DP has become a global pariah and this might be a way to both re-establish themselves as a good citizen and to make billions with a sustainable biofuel.

It seemed like the notebook was the perfect bait for Captain Cannabis who was a hemp guru and a huge fan of sustainable fuels.

"So where's the notebook now?" I asked.

"It's still on the boat," he said with curious certainty.

"How do you know they didn't find it already?"

"Finn, I spent the last five years building a hemp fiber car laminating layers of fiber to create the body. I was able to find fiberglass mats and some resin in Havana then hid the notebook by laminating it into the interior of the boat's hull. The only way they could have found it was to take the boat apart and that clearly didn't happen. I think whoever did the search finally realized the crew didn't know anything about it so killed them. Now the only way to get it was to get me to collect it for them."

"I'm still confused," I said. "Why kill the girl and run the boat into Key West? Why not just kidnap you and force you to show them where the notebook is located?"

Hank sounded dazed and defeated. He simply said, "I have no fucking idea," and was quiet.

"Where are you now?" I asked.

"I'm at my place on Shark Key with my security team. These guys are ex-special forces. Whoever went after the notebook has already killed at least one person and maybe the Captain and first mate. I can't collect the notebook now."

Clearly, it was going to be up to me.

"Okay, tell me where to find it and I'll get it." Then he walked me through the location and the way to dig it out.

~ ~ ~

Going to get this notebook was just plain stupid. If it is DP that is after the notebook, they are going to be watching the boat and the house on Shark Key.

Something about this whole story seemed off: hidden rooms, a long-lost notebook, mysterious formulas, family secrets, money, and murder.

Was the boat really stolen? Could Hank have taken it, killed the crew and Nieve then brought it back to Key West? If others were involved why did they not just keep the boat and tear it apart on some small mangrove island outside the reef? Why bring it into Key West with a murdered girl on board? Now a bunch of alphabet agencies are involved from KWPD, MCSO, DEA, USCG and for all I know ICE and the CIA. Old Island Boatyard could be the most crowded boatyard in history.

What did I really know for sure? A girl was found dead on a sailboat off Wisteria. Hank is an eccentric guy who built a hemp body car to save the planet. The sailboat is on a cradle at a local boatyard. Everything else is either a story or supposition. Before going to search the boat, I needed to learn more. I headed home to do some research.

~ ~ ~

The Internet is an amazing technology and Google is its master. I began by confirming that the sailboat *Kilimanjaro* was, in fact, a charter boat. It turned out it was based in George Town and was owned by its Captain, an old salt named Lon and his wife and first mate Rosie.

Lon and Rosie were a retired couple who divide their time between the Bahamas and New Zealand doing charters in the winter out of George Town. On their website charter calendar, it showed the boat as booked for the last two weeks and due to come off charter this week. I called and left a message on voicemail requesting information. Point one for Hank.

For the next two hours, I did more research on

biofuel, hemp cars, Henry Ford and the Dupree family.

There is significant history of the competition between bio or alcohol-based fuels and petroleum-based fuel. Much supposition pointed to the main driver behind Prohibition in the 1920s being to prevent alcohol being used as a fuel. Who knew?

Heavy alcohol taxes and a smear campaign in Congress funded by the petroleum industry eventually killed alcohol as a fuel in spite of its many advantages. It was only seventy-five years later that ethanol came into use again.

Hemp, as a fast-growing biofuel feedstock that could be used to produce fuel, suffered the same fate in the 1930s with the scare tactics such as the film, *Reefer Madness*. It's one of my personal favorites.

There was suspicion that Dupree and William Randolph Hearst opposed the use of hemp for a variety of reasons. While there was no general agreement, common wisdom had it that Dupree wanted to retain control of petrochemicals specifically leaded gasoline and Hearst wanted control of paper made with wood pulp. In 1937, Congress passed a bill outlawing the production and use of hemp under the guise of the corrupting influence of Cannabis, a strain of hemp used as a drug.

I began to wonder what this notebook Hank found contained. It would be interesting if, in fact, Dupree was researching ways to use hemp as an alternative to petrochemical products. Or perhaps his motive was to keep the formula out of the hands of Henry Ford to preserve Dupree's lock on the petrochemical industry.

While all this was interesting and seemed to confirm many of the background information from Hank, he could have made it all up using the same sources I had just accessed.

I needed to find out if his paranoia about being

followed was real. I needed to go to the boatyard.

As a former EOD operator with Navy Special Forces, I understand the importance of reconnaissance and advance planning. Our mission planning could take weeks for a single operation with redundancies and backup built in for just about every conceivable contingency.

With that in mind, I grabbed Crutch, hopped on my scooter and headed for the boatyard. 'Do as I say not as I do' echoed in my thoughts. Besides, I didn't have weeks, plus my usual backup was in Miami.

As I left, I sent a text to my boss and former BUD/S instructor, Matt Divine. "Investigating possible motive 4 death on boat that struck *Blue Agave*. Going Old Island Boatyard. Determine any bad shit around *Kilimanjaro*. Will call in 3 hours unless in trouble, if no call send backup."

Okay, so it's not exactly standard operating procedure, but it was at least something.

Crutch and I rode up United to White Street then over to Flagler and eventually up U.S. 1 to Stock Island. The Old Island Boatyard is off Shrimp Road.

To avoid disturbing any surveillance that might be in the area, we parked on Macdonald and hiked down 5th going south. Four in the morning is about the best time to approach a target when people are tired and more likely to make mistakes. It was only midnight so I decided to go to the bar at Safe Harbor Marina to get the lay of the land and see if anything unusual was going on in the area. Of course killing some time over a beer sounded like a good idea too.

Charlie the bartender was an old buddy so I ordered a Stella and water for Crutch. He needed to have his wits about him.

Charlie was about as tuned into harbor life as anyone on Stock and we swapped stories about my last adventure at the marina with my ex-wife and her exploits with the Nicaraguan drug dealer Ortega. He asked how things were going with Stacy, the girl I met at the marina, and he told me about the latest excitement with the dead girl on the sailboat *Kilimanjaro.*

"Yeah I heard from OJ about it," I replied nonchalantly. "He said they brought the boat up here."

"Yeah, it's amazing," he offered, "They bring boats up here all the time for repairs but I have never seen one with so much interest in it."

"Interest?" I tried to make my response sound like casual conversation.

"Yeah, I had three assholes in about nine tonight. Shitty tippers by the way."

Note to self. Never tip a bartender too little or too much if you don't want to be remembered.

"Asked about the boat and about security around the yard. I told them about Bill Hartman's two Dobermans that patrol the yard at night." He smiled.

Bill was the owner of the yard. "I didn't know Bill had two Dobermans."

"He doesn't, but I figured they wouldn't know that. Bill is the cheapest son of a bitch on Stock. He wouldn't feed two dogs to protect his mistress much less the yard."

"I don't blame him," I chuckled. "Have you seen his mistress?"

Charlie laughed and asked, "So what dragged your ass up here tonight?"

"OJ offered to let me have a look at the boat so I can have a description for the insurance claim. It was the boat that hit *Blue Agave* and I want to make sure the damage is consistent with what happened to Abacus' boat." *Boy, am I good on my feet.*

"Bit late for that ain't it?" he asked.

"Yeah, I got hung up in town so I figured what the hell, I get it done tonight and file tomorrow."

"Yeah," he said skeptically. "Well watch out for those dogs." He paused. "The human ones I mean."

I thanked him for the beer then headed out to the dock with Crutch when a text from Matt came in.

"Don't be an asshole Finn. Wait for me to get into town. Leaving now."

Needless to say, I ignored his advice and erased all the texts. Given that no one had yet connected me to Hank and I had permission from OJ to look at the boat, I figured the best approach was to simply walk into the yard like I belonged and see who showed up.

Crutch and I walked through the gate about twenty-five yards from the marina dock and began to look for a white boat. *Good luck with that in a boatyard.* After about ten minutes of wandering, I saw a boat with a bunch of yellow police tape around it.

As I walked over, I felt the barrel of a gun press against my neck.

"Don't turn around," said a gruff voice.

I stopped and looked down at Crutch. "Thanks for the heads up Lassie."

He sat down and saluted with his one paw. *Smart ass.*

I started to turn around. "It's okay, I have permission to be here. I'm an insurance investigator for . . ."

"I don't give a shit who you are asshole, don't turn around." *I am so good at making new friends.*

I kept turning. "No, you don't get it."

Crutch growled. About time I thought.

"I said don't turn . . ."

I was already halfway through the turn so I swung my right arm up and across to knock the gun away from me, hoping this guy was dumb enough to have looked down at Crutch when he growled.

He was.

It was not my smartest move, but he was a bit flat footed and my left roundhouse punch benefited from my turn momentum and caught him right on his TM joint. It usually either broke or dislocated a jaw causing intense pain and disability.

This guy was tough and it took my right elbow to his nose as I swung back to put him down. The gun fell from his hand and he folded up, down for the count.

A voice in the dark whispered quietly, "Carl, you okay?"

"Yeah," I whispered as I picked up the gun. "Stray dog." It's hard to distinguish voices in a whisper.

"Okay, but keep it down," came the response.

I knelt down and patted Crutch then searched Carl for ID. All I found was a business card for Carl Wallace, 'Special Operator for Blunt Force Security' and a wad of cash. This guy was clearly not the 'A' team; maybe not even the 'B' team.

I dragged his unconscious body, all three hundred plus pounds of him, behind a stack of paint drums where he had probably been hiding. You need to ease up on the burritos pal I thought as I dragged him. I posed him like he was sleeping, and pulling his ball cap down over his eyes. It might buy a second or two if someone came looking for him.

If it was the same three guys in the bar that were out here now, then at least they were down by one.

I figured since my little 'I'm just a simple insurance guy' worked the first time, I'd try it again. I tucked the gun, kindly donated by Carl, behind my back, covered it up with my shirt then again began walking toward the *Kilimanjaro*.

This guy was a little smarter. He simply tried to cold cock me with his gun. Crutch seemed to have learned his lesson and swung into action and bit the guy on his leg. I turned in time to see the gun pointed toward Crutch.

I yanked Carl's gun out and pointed it at Contestant Number Two.

"Freeze asshole," I whispered. "Drop the gun."

"Fuck you, drop yours or I'll shoot the dog."

"Go ahead, I can get another one but you'll be dead," I said in a voice that was barely audible.

Crutch's highly evolved ears heard it and he seemed to do a double-take as if to say, "What the fuck dude?"

My lights went out when I assumed Contestant Number Three caught me behind the ear with a blunt object, probably the butt of his gun.

CHAPTER SIX

The fact that I awoke as the sun came up was in itself a miracle. If I fool them once shame on them; if I fool them twice, they really are stupid.'

I tried to sit up to see where I was but I seemed to have a weight on my chest. Looking down I found a body lying across me with a combat knife stuck in its neck. As I turned my head and again tried to orient myself, I saw a police officer coming toward me with his gun pointed at me.

"Stay where you are and don't move!" he yelled.

A bit redundant I thought but under the circumstances not totally unwarranted.

I lay still.

He leaned over and put his left hand on the neck of the body on top of me and felt for a pulse.

No pulse.

"Can you get this dump truck off me? I can hardly breathe," I wheezed.

"As soon as another officer gets here, we will move him," he growled.

As I started to look around me I saw that blood had leaked over me. His body lay over my left arm and body, his head hung face down on my right side.

A minute later, two more police cars arrived and from the sounds of sirens, more were on their way.

The first cop began taking pictures with his cell

phone to preserve the scene and the two other officers slowly dragged the body of the man on top while the other held his gun pointed at me. Once the body was moved off me I was rolled over and handcuffed.

"Look, Officer, I came up here early this morning to inspect a boat that crashed into my client's boat on the moorings off Wisteria. I am an insurance investigator." The two officers pulled me up.

"Name?" one said.

"Finn Pilar," I replied. "Have you seen my dog?"

"Mr. Pilar, what happened here?" he asked.

Being an ex-cop, I knew the drill. "Am I under arrest?" I asked.

"Should you be?" he responded.

"No," I replied in my most convincing tone.

"Mr. Pilar, can you tell me what happened here?"

"I am not really sure. I came out here last night to look at the boat that rammed my client's boat. I had a beer at the marina bar then walked over to the boatyard. The next thing I remember is waking up this morning with a very sore head, a body on my chest and you pointing a gun at me. If you don't believe me, you can ask the bartender. "

Okay, so I may have left out a few details but it was early days.

"Do you recognize the man lying on top of you?" he asked.

"How could I?" I asked. Better to answer a question with a question.

"It was dark last night and I was focused on finding the boat. How would I recognize anyone, even my own mother?" *Sorry, Mom.*

"Is that your knife in his neck?"

"What knife?" I replied. "All I could see was a big guy lying on top of me."

"Mr. Pilar, you are doing a good job of not

46

answering my questions."

"Officer, I spent eight years in the KWPD and understand my rights and responsibilities. I am trying to be helpful." I pleaded, "Are you going to arrest me or detain me as a material witness? In either case, you need to give me a Miranda warning. Until then, am I free to go?"

A familiar voice over my shoulder asked, "Officer, this man done something?"

I craned my neck to see OJ walking toward us.

"OJ, would you tell 'Officer Friendless' here who I am?"

"Finn, shut the fuck up and answer the man's questions," he replied sounding a little more than pissed.

Duly chastised, I responded, "Okay Officer, you got me. Take me in." All right, so I was not completely duly chastised.

Officer Friendless looked at OJ, then at me, then at OJ, indecision written all over his face. Finally, good sense prevailed and he undid the handcuffs.

"Don't leave town," he mumbled and left me in order to direct the newly arrived EMTs about dealing with the crime scene.

I turned to OJ and said, "New guy?"

OJ still looking pissed didn't bother to answer my question and said, "Off the record Finn, what the fuck happened here?"

It was time to share a little to get a little.

"Before I get into that, how is it that you guys came out here so quickly?"

"We had a call from your buddy, Matt Divine saying you had missed a check-in call with him and he was concerned. Now give it to me straight. What the hell happened here?"

"To be completely honest," I began, although I

truly hate that phrase as it implies that otherwise, I was not being completely honest. *On second thought, that is often true in my case.*

"To be completely honest, I am not entirely sure. I came out here last night with Crutch . . . . Wait a second, where's Crutch?"

"Oh yeah, animal control picked him up early this morning wandering in the Marina. He's down at the SPCA."

Crutch must have been really pissed about my comment that it was okay to shoot the dog and I could get another one.

"I need to go pick him up now," I said hoping for a little time to get my thoughts together.

"After we talk," said OJ with not an ounce of empathy.

"All right, all right," I began. "After we met last night, I decided that I should probably look at the *Kilimanjaro* sooner rather than later. It struck me as strange that a perfectly good boat would be left to drift into Key West."

"I went home and did some research on Google. It seems that the *Kilimanjaro* was, in fact, a charter boat out of George Town in the Bahamas owned by a captain and his first mate. It was on a two-week charter." I could see a light go on for him.

"So you think the other two blood spatters might be the Captain and his mate," he said.

"Exactly," I confirmed. "I called the number listed on their website and just got a voice message, although that doesn't necessarily mean anything is wrong. It simply raised the stakes in my mind. What could be worth potentially killing three people?" I mused.

"I came out here around midnight and had a beer at the marina bar. Charlie, the bartender told me that three guys were asking about the boat so I figured I would go check it out. The last thing I remember was a guy standing in front of me with a gun, then waking up to Officer Friendless pointing his gun at me telling me not to move."

"Finn, I have known you a long time and even on your worse day you're not that stupid or that easy to get the drop on."

"Thank you," I replied smiling at the compliment. "Maybe I am just getting old," I said immodestly.

"It wasn't a compliment. You're leaving something out."

There's a problem with having a history with someone; they know you too well.

"Okay, while I was approaching the boat, a guy came up behind me and stuck a gun to the back of my neck. I took him down with a left to the jaw and an elbow to the face but as I was searching him for ID I was hit from behind. That's the last thing I remember."

"Did you recognize him?" OJ asked.

I paused.

"Give." said OJ with a 'don't give me any bullshit' tone.

"Yes, he was the guy on top of me when I woke up, but I didn't kill him."

I could tell OJ was trying to sort out the story and I had given him enough for him to believe I was being truthful. I waited.

"Empty your pockets," he finally said.

Shit. "OJ, are you going to arrest me?" I asked.

"Empty your pockets," he repeated sternly.

"OJ, you know that anything you find there will be inadmissible unless you read me my rights," I offered.

"Empty your pockets," he repeated again.

"OJ this is an illegal search and I object!" I said with emphasis on the 'I object'.

"Officer Friendless, I mean, Fredricks, come over

here please," he called out to the original cop.

When he came over OJ said, "Officer please read this man his rights."

Officer Friendless smiled, "You have the right...blah, blah, blah. Do you understand these rights?"

"Yes," I replied.

"Please cuff and search this man, officer," said OJ.

With renewed enthusiasm, Officer Friendless took out his cuffs.

"Officer, before you cuff me, do you mind if I empty my pockets first? As much as you might like to grope around down there I would prefer to fondle my own package."

The smile left his face and he blushed. *New guys are so easy to bait.*

Getting serious, he pulled out his gun, pointed it at me and said, "Turn around and place your hands behind your back." He cuffed me and turned out my pockets laying my wallet, money clip, seventy-five cents in spare change on the hood of his car.

OJ looked at me and said, "Where is it, Finn?"

"Where is what?" I replied looking at him innocently.

"Your combat knife. A Microtech Scarabe DE if I remember correctly," he said. His memory was too long.

"Now that you've read me my rights, I would like my lawyer," and at that point, I shut up. Now I knew where to find the knife that was missing from the pocket where I normally carry it.

Officer Friendless pushed me none too gently into his squad car and we drove to the station at Roosevelt and Eisenhower. After being processed and having my shoelaces removed, I was allowed my one phone call then stuck in a holding cell.

Rather than call my lawyer, I started with Matt. "Matt," I began. "How far out are you from Key West?"

"I'd be there by now were it not for the fucking traffic. How do you put up with it?"

"I never drive to Miami," I chuckled.

"Now I know why. Where are you now?" he asked.

"Long story, but I'm about to be put in a cell awaiting either a charge for murder or being held as a material witness."

"Damn Finn, you had a busy night."

"You don't know the half of it," and I gave him the Cliff Notes version of my adventures.

"What can I do?" he asked.

"I need you to do three things for me. First, pick up a steak at Publix then pick up Crutch at the Animal shelter. Give him the steak. He had a rough night. Then take him to stay with a friend of mine on Shark Key. His name is Hank." I gave him the address.

"Second, call Stacy and see if she can get down here and get me released on bail, and third, see if you can track down a company called *Blunt Force Security*."

"Say that name again," he asked.

"*Blunt Force Security*."

"Damn Finn, what does this have to do with them?"

"The guy who jumped me last night had their business card in his pocket. It said his name was Carl Wallace. I suspect the other two guys who were with him were also from Blunt Force."

"I don't know what you are mixed up in Finn, but these guys are bad news. Blunt Force is a military contracting firm that hires ex-special forces operators for a variety of jobs generally overseas. What they are doing operating in the States I don't know."

I thought about it, then offered, "Maybe with the war over there at a low point they are now doing work in the U.S. as well."

"Yeah, that is a possibility."

"They're run by a guy named Edwin King who's an ex-SEAL and son of a wealthy California family. Blunt Force made millions in the *Sandbox* providing security to diplomats and other U.S. personnel during reconstruction in Iraq."

"What's your connection?" I asked.

"Edwin and I were in BUD/S together. We called him 'Whiner' as he never shut up about being hurt or about his rich family. He finished last in the class and even with that I think some guys helped him through in return for cash."

Sounding disgusted, Matt said, "He's like the guy who graduated last in his class at Harvard Medical School but they still call him Doctor."

"Whiner was a *Vanilla SEAL* who was always looking for ways to get out of duty. Nobody wanted him on their team. I lost track of him after his six-year contract was up but I heard he started Blunt Force."

"Okay thanks, that's helpful. When I get out and we can talk without bars between us, I will give you more on this case. In the meantime, take good care of Crutch and tell Hank we will be using his place as a base of operations." I thanked Matt and went back to my cell to wait.

CHAPTER SEVEN

Sitting in a cell does have at least one benefit; it gives you time to think. I was ninety percent sure I hadn't killed Carl, the question was who had and why? I was knocked out with Carl's gun in my hand pointed at someone else while Carl was unconscious behind some barrels. Unless of course, I killed him rather than knocking him out. Digger would be able to tell when he did the autopsy.

Somebody killed Carl and tried to make it look like I did it. They used my knife and put him on top of me. But why? They could just as easily have killed me or taken me hostage. Maybe the cops arriving interrupted them.

In the absence of any more information, I decided a nap was in order. For some reason being knocked unconscious is not a substitute for sleep so I need to catch a few *zzzzz*s.

I awoke as they brought in lunch if you can call it that. The lockup is not known for its cuisine but I hadn't eaten since dinner with OJ so Spam on Wonder Bread with Lime Jell-O pudding was going to have to do. *I should have asked Matt to get two steaks.*

I had missed my morning swim so I did a Crossfit WOD; burpees, pushups, lunges, leg raises, squats and pull-ups. Then rinse and repeat for twenty minutes.

Just as I was finishing up having worked up a good

sweat, Officer Friendless came in, cuffed me and we went down to the interview room.

To my surprise and delight, Stacy was there with OJ.

"Of all the gin joints in all the world, she walks into mine. We have to stop meeting this way," I said to her grinning. "It took you long enough."

"Fuck off Mr. Pilar and shut up," she replied with a smile on her face.

OJ piped in, "Sorry to put a damper on your warm reunion, but I need to ask Finn some questions."

Stacy immediately jumped in with, "Has my client been charged with a crime? If not, you've no right to hold him and I would like him released at once."

"Okay," he said.

We both stared at him.

"Just kidding," he smiled.

"We're holding Finn on suspicion of aggravated assault, homicide, possession of an illegal weapon and trespassing on private property," he said sounding way too serious.

"You left out littering given the body you found on top of me," I offered. "Just trying to be helpful."

Stacy looked at me. "Finn you've been a busy boy. And how many times do I have to tell you to SHUT THE FUCK UP."

She then smiled sweetly at OJ and said, "I've just instructed my client not to answer any questions until we've had time to confer."

OJ sighed, "Fucking lawyers." He got up and left.

"When this is over you know you're going to have to buy him dinner, right?" I said to Stacy.

"Fucking detectives," she snapped. "He's going to have to get over himself."

She leaned over and kissed me. With the handcuffs attached to the table I was somewhat limited in my response but after a minute or so we came up for air.

"So big boy, what's up?"

I took this as an invitation to talk although the innuendo was much more inviting.

I gave her the Reader's Digest version of events from the previous night including the Blunt Force Security part of the story.

"This is a pretty solid frame up," she said.

"You're not being helpful" I replied.

"No problem," she said. "I'll talk to Digger and get him to rush the autopsy to determine the cause of death. I'll also get a bail hearing for tomorrow morning."

I must have looked dejected.

"It's only one-night big boy, you can cope. Suck it up," she smiled seductively.

"That was not what I was thinking of sucking."

"Nor was I," she grinned. "Now before you get any more ideas, remember, Shut the fuck up" and with that, she got up to leave.

"Stacy, thanks for coming down. I really appreciate it."

She kissed me on the cheek. "No need for any additional excitement. At least for tonight," she purred, leaving open the possibility for tomorrow.

"Call Matt and he can take you up to Hank's house on Shark Key. It's bigger than Catherine Street and we can work out of there."

"Hank, your crazy hemp car buddy?" she said surprised. "What's he got to do with all this?"

"Wait till I get out and I'll walk you through the whole story. I need to get Matt up to speed as well."

"Jesus Finn, for one guy on a small island, you sure know how to attract trouble."

With that, she turned, banged on the door and left but not before turning to blow me a kiss. It was going to be a long night.

~ ~ ~

Dinner was Beef Bourguignon with asparagus tips and roasted fingerling potatoes chased with a fine Oregon Pinot.

Just kidding.

Actually, it was Hormel Beef Stew, soggy crinkle fries and lima beans with a diet Coke but I could fantasize.

I ended up making it an early night and woke about five and did another round of Crossfit prison style finishing just in time for crepes with a raspberry-infused crème fraise, caramelized black pepper bacon, and an espresso.

More like powdered eggs, fried spam, cold Wonder bread toast, and powdered coffee also cold.

At eight o'clock the police van picked a group of us up for the ride to the County Courthouse on Whitehead for bail hearings.

Stacy was in court and when my case was called, the Assistant DA outlined the pending charges against me.

"Your honor," Stacy then began. "My client is a highly regarded citizen of Key West and a licensed insurance investigator. He was at the boatyard to inspect a boat involved in a collision with a boat belonging to one of his clients. He had permission from the detective investigating an apparent murder on the boat to examine the boat."

She continued in her usual brilliant way, "While entering the boatyard, he was attacked by a person or persons unknown whom he disarmed and rendered unconscious. While searching for that man's ID, he was attacked again and knocked unconscious. When the officers arrived, he awoke to find himself under the body of a man, who upon examination by the police was deceased.

In this case your honor, my client is the victim of first one then a second vicious assault and now a third at the hands of the police by his being arrested and held in custody."

I love it when she talks lawyer.

"As a citizen with deep roots in the community and who is not a flight risk, I request that he be released immediately on his own recognizance."

The ADA stood up. "Your Honor, Mr. Pilar is a person known to the police community and this court as a disgraced former law enforcement officer and a man of questionable character. He has been associated with known criminals and it is not his first time as a guest of the county."

This guy, I did not like at all.

"Mr. Pilar broke into the boatyard and appears to have attacked a security guard causing him severe bodily injury. The guard was subsequently found in the company of Mr. Pilar stabbed in his neck with a knife believed to belong to Mr. Pilar."

"Objection your honor," said Stacy in a commanding voice. "In the company of, is very different than having a three hundred pound body pinning him to the ground."

"Sustained. Continue please," said the judge.

"Mr. Pilar faces multiple charges, your honor and we request he be held over in custody while we continue our investigation and determine next steps."

After a brief pause the judge began, "After careful consideration of the arguments, I find insufficient evidence to hold him so I order Mr. Pilar released with a bail of ten thousand dollars pending charges. In addition, he is not to travel further than nineteen miles from Key West."

As we turned to leave, he called me to the bench and continued, "Finn, try not to be late for the Tuesday night poker game at the Square Grouper this week. I'm trying to make back the money I lost from you last week."

Of course, he made the limit nineteen miles; just enough for me to attend the weekly poker game. *I've always said that it helps to play poker with folks in high places.*

"Okay George, I'll be there but bring plenty of cash." I smiled at Stacy. "I need to pay my high-priced lawyer."

He snorted.

George and I had been poker buddies in a game that took place at a different bar around Key West or a few Keys up every Tuesday and next Tuesday was at Square Grouper. The most you could really lose was about twenty bucks so it was hardly considered high stakes.

As we left the courthouse after arranging bail and getting some brisket at *Bubba's Bail Bonds and BBQ*, Tracy asked, "What the hell is going on and who the hell is Annalee?"

"Shit," I began, "I forgot to call Annalee," then for Stacy's benefit I added, "Annalee is the cousin, but more like a sister, of the girl who was found on Abacus' *Blue Agave*. I met her several years ago in Cuba. She sent some pictures of her cousin and I was to confirm if the girl on the boat was her cousin."

Stacy looked a little skeptical and said, "Uh huh, and how did you connect the dots in this little family drama?"

I hesitated to gather myself. "Well according to Abacus, the girl on the boat had a tattoo on her right breast and I recognized it from my Cuba trip." I paused. "Hang on, that didn't come out right."

"Uh huh," said Stacy.

"What I mean is the tattoo was the logo for a Casa

Particular in Holguin that belonged to Annalee's parents. I called Annalee concerned the girl on the boat might be her."

"So you knew that Annalee had a tattoo on her right breast, how is that?"

"No . . .no . . . no, I just wondered why some girl would have a tattoo on her breast of the name of that Casa Particular."

"Uh-huh," she replied again.

"Listen, there was nothing between Annalee and me, except for one kiss, three years ago." I stopped, seeing the look on her face. I can be an idiot sometimes. "No, not that kind of a kiss, just a peck on the cheek, sort of a brother and sister kind of kiss. *With tongue down my throat, I thought.*

I realized I was just digging a bigger hole for myself so I said, "Stacy, I need to call Annalee to break the news to her that the girl on the boat was her cousin."

"I am happy to have this conversation later but, I need to make that call and, we need to get back to Hank's place and find out more about this notebook that's on the boat."

"Fine!" she said and stomped off to her rented Mustang with me trailing like a puppy who'd peed on the rug and been spanked with a newspaper. *This was not how my fantasy of our evening began.*

We drove along Truman to North Roosevelt and then over Cow Key Bridge toward Shark Key. It was only once we were on U.S. 1 that I noticed a dark Camaro sitting about four cars back that seemed to be pacing us. I had first noticed it as we were leaving the courthouse parking meters when I admired the dark blue color.

"Stacy, can you pull over at the CVS so I can pick up a couple of things?" I asked.

She pulled into the lot about two hundred yards up

the road still giving me the silent treatment. I got out of the car in time to see the Camaro drive by. Paranoia I guess, and I went into CVS picking up a toothbrush, toothpaste, and Brut deodorant, her favorite smell. I'm ever the optimist.

I got back in the car and after we pulled out of the lot, I saw the Camaro pull out of a driveway as we sped by. The windows were darkened which is not uncommon for a Florida muscle car, but I made a mental note of the plate and rental sticker.

We drove on and the Camaro continued to shadow us until we turned into the Shark Key gated entrance. We rang through to Hank to let us in as the Camaro continued on up the highway past the entrance to the Shark Key enclave.

It had been a while since I had visited Hank at his place on Shark Key. The garage appeared to have been extended a good sixty feet right to the edge of his corner lot. As he came out with Matt to greet us, I couldn't help commenting on the expansion.

"Yeah, the neighbors hated it but I slipped a few bucks to the HOA President and the Board went along," he replied confidently.

For Hank, a few bucks probably paid for a new sea wall around the island but what's the point of being rich if you can't add some garage space?

"Why the hell do you need that much garage space?" I inquired.

"You'll see," he replied enigmatically.

I greeted Matt with a bear hug and thanked him for his help.

"Finn at this rate, I am going to have to move down here just to keep an eye on you," he chuckled. "I thought this was a sleepy little backwater but you're turning it into a weekly gunfight at the O.K. Corral"

"Hey, I live here so I can ride around on my bike

with Crutch, swim and drink Bloody Mary's before noon. Speaking of Crutch . . . "

In yet another fantasy, I expected my three-legged *Lassie* to come bounding up to me and give me a big sloppy doggy kiss. Instead, as I scanned the room, I spotted him lying under a table in the hall. I called his name, he opened one eye, turned his head, rolled over and farted. *Mental note to self: no more steak for him.*

"Bad night dude?" I asked.

Matt answered for Crutch. "He seemed pretty pissed having to spend part of his day in Doggy Lockup. Based on that smell, prison food does not agree with him." *Well, that makes two of us I thought.*

We left Crutch to nurse his grievances and retired to the deck overlooking the ocean while Hank fired up the grill.

"I imagine you could use some decent food after your night at *Chez Ile du Diable*," Hank offered. "I pulled some steaks from the freezer and had Consuelo put together wedge salads with her homemade Gorgonzola dressing."

Consuelo is Hank's Cuban housekeeper/ chef/bodyguard who has been with him for the last several months. Rumor has it she was a former Cuban Special Forces Operator who came to America to get a sex change operation. Based on her build, I would never want to see her pull out her gun.

We drank Bucaneros while waiting for the steaks to cook then we feasted. Hank broke out a nice Stags Leap Cabernet to go with the steaks. Feeling well fed and with a cold beer in hand, I decided it was time to find out what was really going on.

CHAPTER EIGHT

Hank, Matt, and Stacy gathered on the dock while I reviewed my experience at the boatyard.

"Hank, I think it's time for you to come clean. What the fuck is going on?"

Hank stood up and said, "Rather than tell you, let me show you," and he directed us to his new garage. As we walked he began, "Most of you know that I spent the last five years designing and building a custom sports car built with a hemp fiber body."

I jumped in. "We know Hank, we've seen you speeding around town in your *Smokin' Hot Hemp Car*. What's your point?"

"Let me finish," he said sounding testy. "Scientists today have irrefutable evidence that petroleum-based fuel consumption is seriously damaging, even potentially destroying our planet. There are some who deny it. Most of these are political hacks in bed with the fossil fuel industry. We live in a world of 'fake news', misinformation and corporate lobbying. Corporations have a profit motive and politicians have a re-election motive. It's the rest of us who suffer."

I had to stop him. "Hank, I love you man, but you are starting to sound like a member of the tinfoil hat crowd."

He laughed, "Finn, my objective is simple. I want to make burning fossil fuel of any kind, similar to the attitude towards smoking. As you know smoking has become, at least in many places, totally socially unacceptable. We have No Smoking signs in most restaurants, warnings on cigarette packages and no smoking in public buildings, even some beaches."

He had our attention.

"Imagine if cities had no petroleum fuel allowed within the city limits, warning signs on petroleum fuel stations and carbon negative building materials required in all public works projects."

I'd known that Hank was a man with big dreams but this was 'change the world' stuff.

He continued, "My research has been able to demonstrate that by using biofuel and hemp fiber, we can make and run not just carbon neutral vehicles but we can make them carbon negative, meaning they will actually take carbon out of the atmosphere."

With infectious enthusiasm, he emphasized, "We literally could save the planet!"

We finally reached the door to the garage. As Hank leaned down to put his thumb on the biometric lock to open the door, a shot rang out and a hole appeared in the door where his head had been a second before.

Matt hit the door as it sprang open shoving Hank in with him diving for the floor. I followed a second later pushing Stacy in after them and falling on top of her.

Several other shots followed us but they were above us as we lay on the concrete. I kicked the door shut and heard the sound of an M4 opening fire. With a glance through the window of the garage, I could see a high-speed racing boat tearing away about a quarter mile offshore with Consuelo, rifle in hand trying to hit it before it was out of range.

Matt and I looked at each other.

It appeared that somebody did not like whatever

Hank was doing and seemed ready to kill to keep it from happening. Climate change denial was one thing but climate change life denial was something else.

Matt was on the phone immediately. "Dale, it's Matt."

"Hey, Robo, wha's up?"

"Do you still keep a QRF on the east coast?"

"Sure where are you?"

"Key West."

"What do you need?" Dale asked.

"Round the clock protection. We're facing an unknown force so I need you here yesterday."

"I can have a six-man team there in three hours and six more in twelve."

"Perfect, gun up. Here are the location coordinates. See you soon," said Matt before hanging up.

I looked at Matt quizzically and he explained, "Dale Baldwin is CEO of the WWF."

"Clearly not the World Wildlife Foundation or the World Wrestling Federation . . . "

"Not even close. It stands for Worldwide Weapons Force. Dale is an ex-Marine Force Recon Colonel who I use on a contract basis for high-stakes protection of our clients. After you mentioned Blunt Force and with the apparent interest in Hank, I figured we could use some help."

Hank and Stacy sat silently on the floor looking stunned. I asked Hank, "Who else do you have here besides Consuelo who has a gun and is trained to use it?"

He did not respond at first so I tapped him on the shoulder and asked again, "Hank, who else do you have here besides Consuelo who has a gun and is trained to use it?"

He seemed to come out of his daze and said, "I have a gun safe in the back corner of the garage. I've got an

H&K MP 5, a .300 Win Mag Sniper rifle plus a pair of Glock 19s. Consuelo has an M4 but you know that already, and another Glock."

"Jesus Hank," was all I could say. He had quite the arsenal for a tree hugger.

I reached over and touched Stacy on the arm. She pulled back in apparent surprise, then smiled and took my hand. I guess we had at least a mini-truce after her snit about Annalee.

"How the fuck did they find us?" asked Matt.

"My bad," I replied. "When we were driving here from the courthouse earlier I thought we might have been followed."

Stacy looked at me, "Oh?" was all she said.

"I had Stacy stop at the CVS so I could see if the car would stick around and it did. It followed us again and saw us turn onto Shark Key."

"I got the plate so we can call it in but I honestly didn't expect they would just start shooting. They must have seen us on the deck during dinner and figured out where we were staying."

Matt jumped in, "So why were they shooting at us? Were they after you, or Hank?"

I'm sure the look on my face conveyed that I had no idea.

Hank, on the other hand, looked as guilty as a puppy who'd left a dump on a pricey Persian rug.

"I expect it's me," he began. "They have not been able to find the notebook so I think they may figure the next best thing to do is eliminate me so no one can have access to it."

This was all too much for Matt. "Hank, what the fuck is going on and who are THEY?"

After a brief pause, Hank walked over to the wall and flipped on a light switch, then turned and pointed behind us.

There standing on a rack was a forty-eight foot catamaran ocean racing boat.

Key West is the home of the Super Boat World Championships held each fall. Sponsors like GEICO Insurance, Lucas Oil, and Dupree Petroleum have most recently dominated this highly competitive sport.

"Damn," I said to no one in particular. "Dupree Petroleum."

I recalled that last year in the Super Boat Unlimited Class, the World Championship winner was a catamaran sponsored by Dupree Petroleum.

"Hank, no more bullshit, what's this about?"

Hank seemed to gather his thoughts and began, "After I built the hemp car and did the circuit of TV shows and hemp trade shows, I realized I was preaching to the converted. If I was going to truly make a difference, I had to increase the exposure of hemp fiber construction as a quality material that was also competitive with the toughest materials in the world."

"So you built a boat?" I asked with more than a little sarcasm.

"Not just any boat, but one that can travel at over two hundred miles per hour under the harshest conditions, beat the best carbon-based product in the world and actually remove carbon from the atmosphere."

"And?" I tossed out to encourage him and keep him talking.

"Okay, look, Dupree Petroleum has been doing everything it can to rebuild its reputation after the disastrous five million barrel Gulf oil spill in 2010. They've spent millions on advertising its sustainability and environmental commitments. It was the worst oil spill in history and ultimately cost them over sixty billion with a 'B'.

He sighed and continued, "After only seven years

it's all but forgotten and the new political administration are already rolling back regulations to reduce the possibility of another spill."

"Hank, get off the soap box and back on point please," I threw in.

"That IS the point!" he shouted. "Dupree is using its team sponsorship of Super Boats to reassert its commitment to fossil fuels and carbon-based fiber in construction. Because I share the Dupree name, I want to use a boat built of hemp fiber and titanium mesh, fueled by biofuel made from hemp to defeat the Dupree racing boat at the next World Championships."

Looking down to avert his eyes from our dubious stares, he went on. "If I can defeat them at their own game, I can demonstrate the viability of sustainable hemp-based materials and fuel. In addition, I can clear the Dupree name for generations to come."

"Why do you think you can win?" I asked.

"This boat is built of hemp fiber and titanium mesh. It is twenty percent lighter than traditional carbon fiber boats, thus can use twin 1250 horsepower engines powered by hemp biofuel to deliver greater acceleration. Finally, it has a more balanced weight distribution and less drag in the water. It is capable of two hundred and thirty miles per hour and accelerates ten percent faster out of the turns."

The three of us just had our eyes focused intently on Hank to not miss a word and digest what he was telling us.

"This boat can prove that the world need not be dependent on fossil fuels to achieve cost effective, carbon negative, high-performance results."

I waited for the heavens to open and a choir of angels to sing the *Hallelujah Chorus*.

Hank was clearly an evangelist for sustainability with hemp being the material of choice. My question, although the answer seemed apparent, was "So who do you think is trying to stop you?"

"While I can't prove it, I think Dupree Petroleum is trying to stop me. I suspect they may have hired this Blunt Force firm to steal the notebook I got in Cuba. Barring that they either want to scare me off or if necessary, kill me."

"Hank there are some things here that don't make sense to me," Stacy jumped in after listening carefully to his story.

"Dupree is a worldwide company with over fifty thousand employees. They are a huge provider of agricultural chemicals that I would think would be a prime beneficiary of a move to hemp-based fiber and fuel. So my question is, why do they want to stop this now?"

I think I mentioned that she was the smart one in our relationship. *Or the relationship for which I hoped.*

"Stacy," said Hank, "that's a great question and I don't have a good answer for you."

"I suspect the reason is that hemp is a unique plant. It's extremely fast growing, does not require special growing conditions, nor does it require chemical fertilizers or pesticides unlike other sources of biofuel like corn or sugar beets."

Wanting to sound smart, I offered, "So if it became accepted as a fuel, it would reduce demand for Dupree oil reserves and production facilities and not increase demand for its chemicals."

At this point, Matt jumped in. "Look this is all great theory, but I think until WWF gets here we need to *gun up* and establish defensive positions in the event that our friends return."

This seemed to me to be imminently sensible.

We killed the lights in the garage, called Consuelo who came over to the garage through the house, and we barricaded the doors except for the security door we had come in earlier.

Matt and Consuelo discussed next steps.

Matt took operational control and outlined the plan. "We need to have eyes on the coast and on the road so Consuelo has decided to set up a perimeter outside. She is going to take the .300 Win Mag to the second floor of the house and provide 'overwatch' on the ocean side of the house. I will take the M4 with a suppressor and patrol the roadway." Consuelo headed out.

He turned to me, "Finn you take the H&K and one of the Glocks, to cover the inside of the garage. Stacy and Hank will each take a Glock and stay with you."

Finally, he added, "WWF should be here in a little under two hours so let's just make sure we are good until then."

Hank went over behind the boat and pulled away a tarp on the floor. Beneath it was a safe inserted in the concrete with a keypad to open it. He opened the safe and began to pass out the weapons. Matt checked each one and made sure we had extra mags.

After passing out the guns Hank closed and covered the safe. We split up and began to wait.

I went over to Hank and asked him to cover the ocean side windows then I asked Stacy to go with me over to the north wall windows.

"Stace?" I asked. Stace is the name I call her when I know I am in trouble, hoping she thinks it is cute. "When we get out of this little mess can we chat about Annalee? There was nothing between us except a kiss she gave me three years ago for helping her brother in a bit of a jam."

I figured the quicker we settled this the better.

Stacy looked at me and smiled, "Finn, I don't care if she gave you a blowjob while wearing a blue dress as you smoked a Cuban cigar."

"Clinton references, really?" I asked with a high pitch in my voice.

"Okay, just as long as you know this. If you want me, just whistle. You know how to whistle, don't you Finn? You just put your lips together and blow."

"Much better," I said and whistled.

She leaned over and kissed me. I forgot about Annalee's kiss.

When we came up for air, I took a deep breath and said, "I was born when you kissed me." She smiled and replied, "I died when you left me." *Neither of us seemed quite ready to finish that quote yet.*

"Keep your head down and never look out the window in the same spot twice."

I walked over to see how Hank was doing when the window near Stacy shattered as the bullet passed through seeming to graze her in the head.

"No-o-o-o-o!" I screamed and raced back toward her as she fell. Blood was pouring from a wound along the side of her head and she was not conscious.

CHAPTER NINE

Suddenly all hell broke loose as Matt started to fire the M4 toward the street. His three measured shot bursts seemed to be directed at a service vehicle parked by the far corner outside the entrance to Shark Key. It said Rolando's Plumbing – "We Plumb the Depths of your Drain" in faded letters on its side panel.

Stacy groaned as she lay with her head on my lap. I used my shirt to clear away the blood and get to the wound. As the bleeding slowed, I could see that she had been caught by flying glass from the window and not by the bullet.

"Stacy, can you hear me?" I begged.

"Of course I can you idiot, I just hit my head when I fell. Now let me up." *That's my rough and tumble girl.*

"Hang on a second before you get up. You've lost a lot of blood so take it easy."

"What do you mean, blood? she asked then she looked down and saw my shirt drenched in her blood. "Damn," she whispered and fainted.

Matt seemed to have stopped firing and I risked a look out the window. The van was gone and several people began to appear from different houses along the road.

The sound of distant sirens seemed to cause them to scatter and I realized they were probably the undocumented nannies, maids, and gardeners who worked on the yards in the area.

I called over to Hank and told him to take the weapons and put them back in the safe.

Matt and Consuelo came in with their guns. We waited in the garage to get our stories straight before the police arrived.

Just my luck that Officer Friendless was first on the scene. *Do we only have one cop in the Keys?*

Six additional cars started to show up and Key West's one and only *Lenco* Bear Cat SRT vehicle. Eight armored up SWAT guys jumped from the back of the Bear Cat and rushed forward getting into position around the house.

Gunfire on Shark Key is a major event given the amount of money located in this ultra-wealthy private enclave. I sent Hank out to talk to the first SWAT guy he found. His calm demeanor and hands on his head probably reassured them that he was not a threat.

Not so.

They grabbed him, threw him down on the ground and had him flex-cuffed in the blink of an eye. I guess we should be happy they didn't shoot him.

A man in a suit and tie, usually a defendant or a groom in Key West, came up to him and they began to speak. I concluded he was a detective.

After about five minutes, the suit cut the cuffs off Hank and they came toward the garage together.

"Detective Hannigan," Hank said. "My friends and I were here for dinner and I wanted to show them my new boat. We came over to the garage and as I was opening the door a bullet hit the door near my head. My housekeeper Consuelo saw a boat on the water accelerating away at a high rate of speed. We had all ducked into the garage and didn't see it."

Consuelo nodded in agreement, "Si, si Señor , barco muy rapido." Hank looked at her and sent her an eye message that I think said, "Talk English so ICE doesn't show up here tonight too."

Hank continued, "We ran over to the other side of the garage to get as far from the door as possible when a bullet came through the window and hit Stacy."

Stacy right on cue, holding a towel on her head, pretended to be dazed and confused.

"It turned out that she was hit by flying glass from the window," Hank added to help clarify the situation.

"Then a different sounding gun started firing," added Matt, "and suddenly it seemed like a firefight in Ramadi."

Detective Hannigan asked, "How do you know about Ramadi?"

Matt simply said, "I was deployed there," without adding any details.

"I assume someone called the cops because when the shooting stopped we could hear sirens in the distance," Hank continued.

"Were you all in here when the shooting started?" Hannigan asked.

"No, we were outside the door to the garage like I said except for Consuelo who was cleaning up after dinner," replied Hank.

"Could you see who was shooting at you?" he next asked.

I chimed in, "We could see a van with Rolando's Plumbing on its side just outside the Shark Key entrance but I didn't see anyone actually shooting.

Better to stick as close as possible to the truth. It reduces the chance of a screw up later. I figured he would call that in immediately which he did.

"Did you call the police when this started?" Hannigan continued.

Matt jumped in. "No, I called my office to get my security team here as soon as possible." He knew they would be showing up soon which meant more questions from the police.

Hannigan looked confused. "Your security team?" he asked.

"Yes Detective, I run an insurance investigation company, *Divine Interventions,* and one of my clients had his boat damaged by another boat chartered by Mr. Dupree here." He pointed to Hank.

"My investigator in Key West, Mr. Pilar, called me after he was attacked last night while attempting to examine the chartered boat. I came down here to try and figure out what was going on. When the shooting started, I decided to get security down here as soon as possible. They should be here this evening."

"Wait a minute," Hannigan said slowly. "Mr. Pilar, Mr. Finn Pilar?" asked Hannigan.

"That would be me, but no need to stand on ceremony, just Finn is fine," I offered jovially.

"Weren't you in lock up last night for assaulting a security guy at Old Island Boatyard?" he asked scrunching up his forehead.

"That would also be me," I added again. *Just my luck to get a detective who actually reads the daily arrest logs.*

"Detective," began Stacy. "This evening we were shot at and I was wounded by flying glass. We have no idea why and we are concerned for our safety. Can you please arrange for security until Mr. Divine's team arrives."

"And you are?" asked Hannigan checking her out.

"I am Mr. Pilar's attorney," she replied.

"So who do you think was shooting at you?" asked Hannigan, "and for that matter who was shooting back?"

We looked at one another then Matt replied, "That is the sixty-four thousand dollar question."

Stacy looked confused which is very rare. I guess she was too young to remember that one or didn't watch reruns of 50s game shows.

Matt continued, "I think the other question is why? Also was the attack on Mr. Pilar at the boatyard connected with this evening's attack?"

Stacy quietly said, "Detective, I am feeling faint and I would like to lie down."

Hannigan suddenly became solicitous - pun intended - and offered, "Would you like to go to the hospital?"

"No, thank you, Detective, I just need to rest."

"All right, I think we're done here for now but I may have further questions once we've processed the crime scene." And with that Hannigan left the garage and we all escorted Stacy into the house.

I took Stacy up to the bedroom that Hank had assigned us and got a first aid kit from Hank. I cleaned up the cut in her scalp then used a couple of butterfly bandages to close it up. A little antibiotic gel and she was good to go.

I know what you're thinking, but even I wouldn't take advantage of her in this condition. That was until she reached over as she sat on the bed, kissed me then pulled me down.

"Young lady," I said feigning shock and horror. "Are you considering what I think you're considering?"

"Shut up Finn, before I change my mind," she growled.

Being the cooperative and pliable guy that I am, I gently pulled her tank top over her shoulders and then her head being careful to avoid touching the bandages on her scalp. Her bra soon followed, as did my shirt.

"Is this the moment when I should whistle?" I asked playfully.

She smiled, "Just put your lips together and . . .

Ohh," she moaned as I licked the side of her breast then caressed her nipple with my tongue.

Her back arched as I continued to savor her body with delicate tastings. I reached down to remove her shorts only to find that she had beaten me to it. *This girl is good.*

I continued exploring down her belly, her navel and I eventually found what I was licking for. She reached down and took hold of me in her hand. She then, with a level of athleticism I did not realize she possessed, found her way on top of me. Taking me into her mouth I continued to enjoy her thighs and . . . well, you get the idea.

It has been said that you can tell when you have had a great night of oral sex when you wake up in the morning and your face looks like a glazed donut. Now that is truly a calorie free Dunkin' Donut. I would take my donut calories in that way any day.

I am not sure how she did it but we seemed to alternate positions without ever disentangling. We sucked, fucked and licked, then did it all again. *It had been a while.*

We came up for air around eleven o'clock and I realized I was starving. I kissed Stacy and said, "I'm starving. I'm going to check on the security team and see what Hank keeps in the fridge. Can I get you something?"

She reached down between my still naked legs and said, "How about some ice cream and chocolate sauce." She paused then continued, "Never mind. Skip the ice cream and just bring the chocolate sauce. I know the perfect delivery vehicle," she grinned and licked her lips.

I grabbed a robe. "I'll be baaaaack," I said in my best *Ahhhhnold* impersonation.

I headed for the downstairs and almost tripped

over Crutch sleeping in the corridor outside our room.

"Have you been listening the whole time?" I asked him. He stood up and came over to lick my hand.

"Is that your attempt at an, 'I forgive you' lick?" He growled, turned his back and flopped back down.

"Hey I got you out of Doggy lockup, didn't I? Besides, you didn't exactly give me any warning before I got whacked in the boatyard."

Still nothing. "Okay, okay, I'm sorry I said that they could shoot you and I would just get another dog." He stirred at that one.

"I got you steak," I reminded him earnestly. It sounded a bit too much like pleading.

With that, he got up and went over to the bedroom door and bumped his nose against it. A three-legged dog has trouble scratching a door.

"Okay, you can go in when I get back. Let's go down to see about security and get some chocolate sauce."

He cocked his head as if he understood what I said and I swear he smiled. As he led the way to the stairs I reminded him, "Besides you should know it's not easy to replace a three-legged dog who can get beer money from tourists."

He grunted and we walked down the stairs into the muzzle of a Glock sticking out of a shadow.

"Freeze," demanded the shadow. "Hands in the air."

CHAPTER TEN

A disembodied voice from a sofa in the living room said, "It's all right Hector. By the sound of the paws on the tile, it's just Crutch and Finn."

Thank goodness there was then the familiar voice of Matt. "Finn, meet Hector Ramirez. Hector meet Finn Pilar. Hector is head of the security team I called in."

"Hola, Señor. Como esta?" Hector asked me.

"Another of your undocumented hired guns?" I chided Matt.

"Excuse me, Mr. Pilar. I am a fourth generation American, born in Brooklyn. I was speaking Spanish which is just one of the five languages I speak. I was simply modeling the stereotype most people have when they meet someone named Hector." He smiled a toothy grin.

"With a name like Pilar, it would have been more appropriate to say hello in Portuguese. Olá, Señor. Como você está?"

"Enough, Hector, I am sufficiently chastened." I matched his grin as I threw up my hands and admitted defeat.

"Matt said you knew how to take a joke. Actually, my name's Bob and I'm from Wisconsin." Then they both busted a gut.

"OKAY, Bob," I replied. "But from now on, you're Hector to me."

Matt continued to laugh as I went into the kitchen in search of an early morning snack. I rummaged around and found some yogurt and a bagel. With a little butter, cream cheese and some slices of smoked salmon I figured it was enough to eat, but alas, no sign of chocolate sauce.

I took my small feast into the living room and found a bottle of Kahlua in a lacquered liquor cabinet. As I headed back upstairs, Matt called after me, "Finn, shift change for the team is four am so save some energy for your shift." He chuckled knowingly.

"I'm not as good as I once was, but I'm as good once as I ever was," I retorted.

"The operative word is once, dude, once. Get some rest. You'll need your wits about you."

As I walked up the stairs with Crutch at my heel, the weight of the day started to descend. I came into the room to find Stacy curled up in a ball asleep. I set down the snack, took a bite of salmon on the bagel, set my phone for a three-fifty wake-up alarm and curled up beside her. Maybe four hours would be enough.

When the early bars of *La Grange* by ZZ Top broke through my slumber, I managed to hit the alarm stop button before the song hit the opening drum riff. Stacy stirred but did not wake up. *Ahh, the innocence of babes.*

I took a quick shower, then raided Hank's closet and threw on black lightweight tactical pants, a tee shirt, black nylon jacket and a black watch cap. I headed down to relieve Hector.

He reported all was quiet and shuffled off to his room on the second floor. Matt was quietly snoring on the sofa. I checked the inside perimeter then finished my now somewhat dry bagel. For the next three hours, I moved stealthily from room to room checking windows and doors for any sign of intrusion.

The TV in the kitchen was on with the volume turned to low and Consuelo was in the middle of fixing breakfast. I switched over to *Max Tracker*, our most accurate local weather station out of Miami and turned up the volume.

Max was just wrapping up his forecast but I could see the beginnings of a tropical depression about a thousand miles off the coast of Venezuela in the southern Caribbean. It was still thousands of miles away but we were in hurricane season so one always needs to be watchful in the Keys.

Hurricane season in the Caribbean and Atlantic is an annual event between June and November. So far this year things had been relatively quiet with only five named storms and only one was a Cat One when it hit the Carolinas.

It looked like another storm was on its way so we all needed to keep our eyes on the weather.

The house slowly came to life and Matt called a meeting over breakfast with the team members not on duty.

"Now that everyone's here," he began, "I want to set the shift schedules and location assignments."

"Finn, I would like for you to take three guys and go to the boatyard where the *Kilimanjaro* is currently being kept." He paused and looked at me intently. "See if you can find this notebook that Hank is talking about. Until we figure out what this is all about, we can't get ahead of it."

"Hank, you stay here with Stacy, Dale and the three guys from his team."

"I will cover the perimeter with three of Dale's guys and we will let the other three rest for the next three hours."

"Now let's eat and meet back here at eleven hundred hours."

As we tucked into breakfast, it was clear that regardless of what gender Consuela identified as, for a bodyguard she was one hell of a cook.

~ ~ ~

I borrowed Stacy's Mustang and with my new posse, we loaded up with the additional armament brought down on the WWF chopper. The drive to the boatyard was less than fifteen minutes and I explained what I wanted from them.

As I went through the gate, I stopped and dropped off one of the guys to cover that entrance. I next located the *Kilimanjaro* still looking forlorn on a cradle surrounded by yellow police tape. We swung around to park the Mustang on the dockside of the sailboat and had my guy slip behind the car for to cover the dock side. Finally, I had the third member of my security entourage climb with me into the cockpit of the *Kilimanjaro* while I entered the salon.

As I climbed down the companionway of the boat into the salon, it was clear that it had been thoroughly searched; actually, more like torn apart.

It might have been the police looking for drugs on board but they are usually more careful in order to preserve the crime scene and any evidence they find. This looked like it was ripped apart in haste and with no thought to anything other than finding something specific.

As I walked through the cabin, it was clear that every cabin and every berth was demolished. Mattresses shredded, bureaus smashed, carpets torn up, every locker removed and even the holds searched. The only advantage I had was that Hank had told me where to look.

The owner's cabin had a large forward berth with a queen size bed, and bedside tables on each side of the bed. Once clearly a well-appointed cabin, it was now in a shambles. The floorboards had been torn up and the contents of the lockers tossed on the bed. Packages of food, toiletries, kitchen supplies and cases of wine had been removed and the lockers searched. I was starting to worry they might have found what they were looking for.

In the far reaches of the locker under the bed, my flashlight picked up a ripple in the fiberglass mesh finish of the hull. If you didn't know what you were looking for you would miss it. I scrambled into the locker and crawled forward until my hand reached the watertight hatch that separated the anchor locker from the hold beneath the floorboards of the master suite.

I could see the ripple was in fact what looked like a repair to the interior of the hull. I reached for my knife then remembering that I had last seen it stuck in the neck of Carl the Blunt Force operator. I scurried back to the cabin and called for my companion to toss me his knife. A second later a thump about a foot from my outstretched hand caused me to pull it back. I hadn't meant him to throw it so it stuck into the floor.

The knife was a nice Benchmade retractable with a double-edged blade that was razor sharp. Since I needed to replace the one lost in Carl's neck, I thought I should consider this model.

Again scrambling forward, I began digging into the gel coat finish of the hull around the mysterious bulge. After about five minutes of poking, jabbing and stabbing, I was able to slip the blade under the patch of fiberglass and force if away from the hull. Beneath the patch was a black leather three-by-five Moleskin notebook filled with notes and formulas.

Suddenly, the hull of the boat back near the cockpit exploded and gunfire erupted. It felt like an RPG had been fired at the boat to take out all on board. I was inside the bow and protected from the blast but still vulnerable to shots penetrating the hull.

The fire was beginning to heat up my little oasis. Based on the heat at my feet, I was concerned that I could not get out that way.

This was starting to look awkward. It seemed that our opposition had decided if they couldn't have the notebook they would make sure we couldn't either.

Above me, the decking of the master stateroom was heating up, likely burning the bedding. The hatch to the locker holding the anchor was available but incredibly small; I assumed no more that eighteen-by-eighteen inches square. I would have to pull the anchor and at least fifty feet of anchor chain was back behind me before I could try to squeeze into the locker and out of the hatch. I could just imagine the response from the gunmen outside when my head popped up through the anchor hatch. Whack-a-Mole with their bullets and my head didn't feel like a viable plan.

Suddenly the whole boat lurched, dropped about two feet then fell on its port side away from the water.

Apparently, the wooden cradle holding the boat up had burned through, first dropping the boat on its keel then tipping it on its side. The downward trajectory from a height of around eight feet sent a pile of bottles, canned goods, and *Charmin* toilet paper down on my head. That toilet tissue really is *squeezably soft* and saved me from the worst of the Cabernet and Merlot bottles hitting my face. *Thank you, Mr. Whipple.*

The other good news was that when the cradle collapsed, the boat landed bow down lying on its port side with the anchor locker hatch no longer exposed to the gunfire from the water. If I could sneak my way out of the hatch, I might not be seen. I gently released the hatch toggle, opened the locker and began hauling yards of anchor chain and the anchor into the storage locker behind me. Once I had that out of the way, I began to squeeze through the hatchway.

Through the Plexiglas deck hatch cover, I could see wreckage from the cradle burning on the ground. Smoke was beginning to fill the locker I was lying in and the heat was building up uncomfortably. The gunfire had subsided so if I was going to get out of this, now seemed as good a time as any to make my move. As I popped opened the hatch cover, cool air began pouring in. The hull acting like a well-drafted chimney began to suck the smoke out of the locker draining the heat toward the stern of the boat, or whatever was left of it.

As I struggled to get my shoulders out of the hatch, a shot rang out hitting about an inch from my hips. The Glock in my waistband was wedged in the opening. With a surge of adrenaline adding strength and urgency to my exit, I pushed out and up, popping from the hatch and onto a burning timber. I rolled toward the stern dousing any burning clothing and putting the lead keel between the gunfire and my singed body. I reached for the Glock and realized that it was likely still in the locker, torn from my belt when I popped out.

I scrambled back toward the hatch and reached in to retrieve it. Re-armed and pissed off, I began to scan the water's edge for my antagonists. I could see the body of one of my team lying behind some cradle timbers not moving. On my right was the body of my knife-lending partner or at least what was left of him after being in the cross hairs of an RPG. I guess I was going to be able to keep the knife. *Maybe too soon?*

Suddenly, shots rang out from what sounded like an AR-15 directed at the pile of paint drums where I had dumped the unconscious body of Carl the other night. A head popped up and the guy I had dropped off at the marina entrance, fired toward a shed by the dock only to draw further fire in his direction.

I lay on the ground and inched toward the stern of the sailboat looking for a gap I might use to take a shot. The rudder was a dagger style hanging below the stern. It had snapped off during the collapse of the cradle and wedged the boat up from the ground just enough for me to see the shed. I took careful aim and waited for the moment when our opponent came out to play.

I waited.

Nothing.

The fire was still burning above me and beginning to make my position untenable.

Fuck it, I fired at the shed.

A second later, he stepped out to fire at the paint drums and I fired again catching him in the chest. He just stared at the paint drums with a stunned look on his face as he collapsed.

I shifted positions away from the main body of the fire and came out from around the stern of the now engulfed *Kilimanjaro*. While I continued to look at the waterfront I sidestepped over to the paint drums looking for whoever was left of my team.

One was lying on his side cradling his arm. He was bleeding from a wound in the bicep. I pulled off my belt and applied a tourniquet to slow the bleeding. He seemed to be in reasonable shape so I went over to the other team member behind the cradle timbers.

The other appeared to have been grazed in the head but was unconscious. His pulse was strong but he was bleeding badly. Head wounds are real bleeders. He would have a hell of a headache when he came to. I tore a strip off my tee shirt and bound the wound. I made a mental note to get these guys names. After all, they had both saved my ass big time.

I could hear sirens in the distance and sat down to wait for them to arrive. I would have to talk to the city about their response times. I felt like we had been in a gunfight for at least an hour. It was probably only ten minutes, but still.

For the second time in forty-eight hours, I was involved in a pitched battle at the same boatyard. At least this time there would be bodies from the other team and I had witnesses on my side. I wondered if the judge would consider this a violation of the terms of bail from the last altercation. *Well, at least I wasn't more than nineteen miles from Cow Key Bridge.*

I checked to make sure I still had the notebook safely inside the zippered pocket of the lightweight tactical pants I had borrowed from Hank. This could end up being a long night.

~ ~ ~

I decided to call Stacy.

"Hey, babe, did I wake you?"

"Mmmm, no I am just lying here thinking about last night and wishing you were here," she said in a decidedly husky voice. "Where are you and what's that noise?"

"Well here's the thing," I began as the wails of the sirens drew nearer. "I may be about to be arrested again and I could use your help."

"WHAT?" she shouted. "I sleep in for an extra hour and you can't stay out of trouble." She took a breath. "What the hell have you gone and done now?"

"It's a long story but I am at the Old Island Boatyard and the fire trucks are just pulling in with the cops not far behind. Can you get down here and try to keep me out of jail? I promise you, they started it," I said sounding like a school kid talking to a pissed off parent. There was a long silence on the phone. "Stacy?"

"Keep your mouth shut and I will be there in ten minutes."

Firemen leapt from the truck and began pulling hoses off the truck when suddenly an explosion erupted onboard the sailboat. Flames shot up once more and it appeared like the fire had reached a propane tank of the galley stove adding urgency to the already tense situation.

The EMTs arrived and rushed over with a go bag of supplies.

"Well Jaysus, if it ain't me olde buddy Finn Pilar, deep in the shite again. What the fuck hay ye been up te, mate?"

My old friend Steve Roberts is a recent immigrant from the Emerald Isle whose Irish accent was as thick as the marine layer of fog off the coast of Coronado during May gray and June gloom. He and his partner Jim Foley, and yes they are both kinds of partners, began to check me out and treat my burns.

"I can wait, Steve," I brushed them off. "You need to look at the guy over by the pile of cradle timbers who has a head wound and the one behind the paint drums with a gunshot to his bicep."

They immediately split up and ran to the wounded WWF guys. Just then the cops showed up. It appeared that Officer Friendless was off shift and a new guy came walking up to me.

"Can you tell me what happened here?" And then he stopped.

"I know you," he said opening up our chat.

I had no idea where this was going.

"You're the guy with the three-legged dog that performs tricks for drinks at the Green Parrot."

I smiled. This might work out okay.

"You were a cop here a while back, right?"

This could be good I thought, but then a cloud passed over his face.

"Didn't you get kicked off the force?"

I needed to nip this in the bud. "It's a long story officer which I am happy to share at the Parrot over a couple of beers."

He seemed to brighten. "Only if you bring your dog."

"Deal," I offered. Crutch was saving my ass from afar.

"Can you tell me what happened here?" he began again.

"Well. . . . I started but was cut short.

"Mr. Pilar is not answering any questions before I have had time to confer with him, officer. What is your name and badge number?"

He looked at me and asked incredulously, "You've already got a lawyer?"

I shrugged to avoid answering him. I knew Stacy's drill.

She made note of his information and after that, we waited for a detective to arrive. I had my fingers cross it would be OJ.

While we waited, Stacy sat down beside me and asked, "Finn, what the hell happened here?"

I took five minutes to outline the events of the last two hours while slipping her the notebook from my zippered pocket. She listened to the story and just shook her head.

"I leave you alone for two hours and you end up in a gunfight with some mysterious mercenary force, shoot one of them apparently to death and burn a quarter million dollar boat. Does that about cover the details?" she added with more than a little sarcasm.

"In fairness," I interjected, "They were shooting at me first and I was on the boat when they fired an RPG which started the fire."

A couple of minutes later a car rolled up and thankfully OJ got out.

"Finn, what the fuck man? One arrest a week is not enough for you?"

"Stacy, good to see you girl. Are you still involved

with this doofus?"

Stacy started to answer when he said, "Don't answer that." He continued, "Okay Finn, you have two choices. You can answer my questions or I can name you as a material witness and drag you down to the station for questioning. Which do you prefer?"

I looked a Stacy and she said, "I have advised Mr. Pilar to only answer your questions in my presence and if that is okay with you, we can come down to the station voluntarily once Mr. Pilar's burns have been properly treated at Lower Keys Medical. Can that work for you?"

OJ looked frustrated but agreed.

I let Stacy help me up and I walked as shakily as I could to her car and she drove me to the hospital. In the car, she continued her interrogation. "So who are these guys that are going after this notebook and what's in it that is worth dying for?"

I paused and answered as best I could. "I have no fucking idea.

"Hank claims that they are mercenaries for Dupree Petroleum but I can't figure out why they're willing to either kill for it or destroy it."

"Once we finish with the cops and the hospital, we can sit down with him and go through it to see what the big deal is. In the meantime, if you can keep it under lock and key, we can get the rest of this cleared up." I gave her the safe deposit box key from Bank of America and while I waited she ran into the bank to put it in the box before taking me over to the hospital.

For the next four hours, we waited at Lower Keys Medical Center for me to get treatment. It seems my condition was less critical than the two gunshot wounds that Steve and Jim brought in from the boatyard.

It turned out my burns were superficial but I

needed a couple of stitches for a cut I hadn't even noticed during all the excitement. Once treated, we headed down to the police station on North Roosevelt and Eisenhower. I felt like it was becoming a second home.

As we walked in, I stopped. *Oh shit.*

CHAPTER ELEVEN

Standing at the desk talking to the clerk was Annalee, all five-foot-ten and one hundred and twenty-five pounds of fiery Cuban temper on full display.

"Listen you perra gorda, mi hermana is lying in your maldito morgue and I demand . . . demand that you let me see her."

The clerk, my old friend Sylvia who was clearly getting agitated said, "Señorita, the maldito morgue as you refer to it is not here, it is at the hospital. Now if you call me a fat bitch one more time, I will be forced to call an officer to restrain and detain you. Lo entiendes?"

It was clear that this was an escalating situation so I decided to bite the bullet and bring all my diplomatic skills to bear.

Well, maybe not exactly. I took Stacy by the arm and started to back away to get out the door. Stacy not understanding said, "Finn we just got here and you need to talk to OJ."

Sylvia looked up and Annalee began to turn around as I assumed that I was totally screwed. I had forgotten just how beautiful Annalee was in the three years since our last kiss, I mean, our last encounter. I went into damage control mode.

"Annalee?" I queried. "Is that you?" hoping that

Stacy would buy my, 'she meant so little to me that I had forgotten what she looked like' routine.

I heard Stacy mutter under her breath as she jabbed me in the ribs. "Asshole," she growled.

"FINN!" Annalee shrieked. "It is you, thank God, I have been trying to explain to this *perra gorda* that you had called me to try to help and I need to see if the girl in the morgue is my sister and she is being a. . . . "

I held up my hand in the classic stop signal and said in my most mature voice, "Annalee, before you dig a deeper hole for yourself," *and for me, I thought,* "Let's thank the nice lady Sylvia and go outside."

She paused, seemed to think about it, then turned to Sylvia and said, "Muchas gracias," then whispered, "Perra," and turned back toward me to leave.

Now Sylvia and I go back a long time and not the way you're thinking. Although she weighs in at about four hundred and fifty pounds, she is happily married to her fourth husband but she always seems to have an eye out for number five.

I winked at her and said, "Let me take care of this and I'll bring you back a treat." She mouthed a thank you and blew me a kiss. I made a mental note to stop at Dunkin Donuts on my way back to see OJ. *One lady appeased in my life; only two more to go.*

I took Stacy's hand and directed Annalee outside the station to a small park next to the driveway. For those of you who have never faced this *prickly* problem, my first challenge was to introduce Stacy and Annalee. I ran the options through my head as we walked awkwardly to the park.

"Annalee I'd like you to meet: Stacy, my friend *no*; my friend with benefits, definitely *no*; my lawyer, a possibility but might give Annalee the impression that I was available; my fiancée, *no, not there yet . . . .*

Or I could try: "Stacy, I'd like you to meet Annalee,

better; the girl I kissed in Cuba, *no*; the girl I told you about, means we talked about her, so *no*. . . . "

I really suck at this relationship stuff.

Stacy stuck out her hand and said, "Hi, I'm Stacy, Finn's lawyer and. . . . " she smiled, "friend."

Women seem to get this stuff intuitively and Annalee said, "You are a lucky woman. I took a shot three years ago and got rejected."

Stacy smiled, *the turf war over*, my role as the piece of meat that had been fought over was clear. Stacy had established her place. Now they would be thick as thieves.

"Okay girls, let's start over," I began. "Annalee, I am very sorry but I think the girl on the boat was your cousin. The tattoo is definitely the *Cat on the Moon* logo and the photo you sent seems to match. I am truly sorry for your loss."

Annalee collapsed suddenly on the grass, her legs seeming to fold beneath her and she quietly began to sob. I looked on helplessly not quite sure what to do. Stacy, now that their roles had been settled, sat down beside her and held Annalee gently as she wept.

I stood on the lawn looking around and shifting my weight from one foot to the other like a distant relative at a wake, hoping for a diversion or a reprieve.

After about an hour – actually five minutes – Stacy pulled out a pack of tissues from her purse and gave it to Annalee. *Some day I need to look into all the stuff women carry around in those things.*

Slowly I helped both Stacy and Annalee up and we agreed to drive up to the morgue to see her cousin's body. We piled into the Mustang and drove up North Roosevelt back onto Stock Island, past the golf course and over to Lower Keys Medical. I called Digger from the car to let him know we were coming and to meet us in the front.

He met us in the lobby and took us down to the morgue. Stacy went in with Annalee to view the body while Digger and I chatted outside the viewing room.

"You've been a busy guy Finn," Digger chuckled. "I had three bodies brought in today. We're calling it the 'Firefight at the Old Island Boatyard'. Were you Wyatt Earp or Bat Masterson?"

"Knowing you as I do Digger, you've already registered the name as a Twitter handle and you're working on the movie rights."

Digger turned serious for a minute and said, "Finn, you need to be careful. Two of the guys that came in wearing body bags were not alone. Just after they came in we had a couple of 'bad hombres' as our President would say, showing up looking for answers."

"They left really pissed off."

"Who were they, Digger?"

"You're joking, right? I don't know but trust me they weren't pharmaceutical reps bringing donuts, free samples, and business cards. These were guys that looked like your boss Matt Divine, tough, battle hard and dangerous."

"Shit, what did they want to know?" I asked.

"After looking at the bodies, they only wanted to know if I knew you and where I could find you?"

"And you said?"

"That I knew you and to try the *Mockingbird*," he said a little sheepishly.

"Okay, no worries. I'll give Abacus a heads up to keep an eye out for them."

"Digger, was there anything unusual about the bodies they were asking about?"

"You mean other that the bullet scars and burned off tattoos?" he asked innocently.

"What do you mean, 'burned off tattoos'?" I asked a little surprised.

"Not burned off exactly. I usually see this on guys who want to erase the tattoo they got on spring break after a one-night stand at the Rosarito Beach Hotel in Baja. Few wives like to look at *Juanita* whenever she showers with her new husband. They usually get it lasered off before the wedding night."

"So both these guys had had tattoo's removed?"

"Yeah, but the weird part was that they both had the tattoo in the same spot and it was the same size."

"Ever seen it before?" I asked not expecting anything.

"Funny you should ask but yes," and he paused.

"Jesus, Digger don't keep me in suspense."

"Well as you well know from personal experience, back in the sandbox, I had to treat a lot of guys. During Operation Phantom Fury in Fallujah, I saw a steady stream of Marines during the worst of it."

"One particular assault team was in the heaviest shit. I treated three or four guys with a tattoo in the same spot on their chests. It was the Force Recon Skull, with wings, a Drager respirator, two paddles and the words, Swift, Deadly, Silent."

"Digger, I knew guys from Recon and they were great operators. They saved my ass more than once. Are you saying these guys could be ex-Force Recon?"

"Not necessarily, but the bodies have burned off tattoos in the same location as the guys I treated as well as battle damage stuff I used to fix up."

I shook my head. "God I hope you're wrong."

I thanked him and went to meet Stacy and Annalee.

~ ~ ~

Annalee was pretty shook-up so I suggested we take her back to Hank's place before Stacy and I went back to meet with OJ who I was sure was beginning to get pissed.

As we drove the short way up U.S. 1 to Shark Key, I

gave Annalee an abbreviated version of the story then asked, "So how did you end up here given how hard it is to come to the States from Cuba?"

"As soon as I heard from you, I started to piece together what happened at the Cuba end," she began. "At first it looked like it was pure coincidence that Nieve was on the boat. Her friend Lisel runs an agency that provides crews for boats that are new to Cuban waters. Lisel called Nieve two days before the boat was set to leave and asked her to fill in.

"I called Lisel after your call and found out that the crew member who was supposed to be on the boat got a call to take a modeling assignment in Havana. When she got to Havana there was an envelope at the hotel with two hundred and fifty dollars and a note to wait at the hotel for further instructions. She waited until the next day when she got a call from someone claiming to be the photographer who said the photo shoot had been postponed but she could keep the money. Cancellations aren't that unusual so she didn't worry about it as she had been paid for her time."

I thought about this for a second and Stacy beat me to it when she asked, "Do you know why Lisel picked Nieve to fill in rather than someone else?"

Annalee paused, "That was the really weird part. Lisel said the captain asked for Nieve."

"What!" I exclaimed. "He asked for her?"

"Yes, Lisel said the original crew member suggested Nieve."

"It seemed a little weird but I didn't think much about it at the time. Now I am not sure what to think," said Annalee.

I did a quick recap. "So you are saying that after accepting an assignment to crew on a boat, the previous crew member - what's her name by the way?" I asked.

"Cristina."

"Okay, Christina calls Lisel to cancel. Lisel calls the captain of the *Kilimanjaro* who says Christina had called him and recommended Nieve as a replacement."

"Yes," she replied.

Stacy jumped in again, "Wait a minute, that makes no sense. If he wanted Nieve for crew to begin with, why not just call her directly to see if she was available?"

I thought about this for a minute.

"Suppose we have this backward. Suppose the Captain doesn't know Nieve at all but somebody, let's call him *Bad Hombre* for the moment, does know her or of her." I stopped to let them catch up.

"Let's say *Bad Hombre* knows Hank has chartered *Kilimanjaro*. He then arranged for Nieve to crew the boat but wants it to appear to be a coincidence. He instructs the Captain to arrange for a crewmember from the local agency. Then two days before the crew pick up, *Bad Hombre* calls Cristina and offers her a modeling assignment. Once that is done, the *Bad Hombre* calls the Captain to cancel Cristina and suggested Nieve. Then the Captain calls the agency and says his crew has canceled but Nieve was suggested to him by Lisel. "Tada, Presto, Bingo! Nieve being on the boat appears random."

"Tada, Presto, Bingo?" says Stacy. "Who are you, Penn or Teller? That is the most convoluted story I've ever heard. Why would they want only Nieve on the boat?"

"I have no idea. This is just a working theory that somebody wanted her on the boat and for it to appear random."

We were pulling up to the house as my phone rang.

"Where the fuck are you Finn?" shouted OJ into my ear.

It was OJ. Shit, I needed to give him a special ring tone so I could avoid his calls. Maybe *Jailhouse Rock* or *Folsom Prison Blues*.

"I'm at the spa getting a Mani/Pedi. I wanted to look my best for my interrogation. What's up?"

"Get your ass down here, like yesterday or I'm going to drag you here in cuffs, put you in a dark cell and beat the shit out of you. Capisci?"

"I love it when you talk dirty," I laughed. "I should be there in fifteen minutes. On second thought, make it thirty. I need to walk Crutch first."

Crutch who had run up to the car when we pulled in gave me one of his signature, 'Sure throw me under the bus' looks and hopped into the back seat.

Matt came out to meet us and I introduced him to Annalee. After a brief explanation of the events and a request to keep Annalee safe, Stacy, Crutch and I drove again back onto the Rock to meet with OJ. We made a quick stop on Roosevelt to pick up a dozen crullers and fritters at Dunkin' Donuts so I could drop them off to Sylvia as we entered the police station.

Once parked at the station, I introduced Crutch to several new trees and shrubs. He marked his new territory and we headed into face the 'Wrath of OJ'.

I waved to Sylvia and put the donuts on the counter. She opened the box, grabbed a fritter and in three bites inhaled it, then smiled. She blew me a kiss as I walked toward the back of the station and OJ's office, Crutch at my heels and Stacy following us, shaking her head.

I knocked on the doorjamb and opened his door as he put down the phone.

"Finn, how many times do I have to tell you to wait at the front desk for me to come and get you? This is a restricted area."

"Okay, fine," I said as I turned around and walked

back to the desk as he shouted behind me, "Finn, you are truly an asshole."

I walked up to the desk and took a fritter and cruller from the box that was now half empty. Stacy took the cruller. I took a bite of fritter and we waited.

OJ waited a petulant five minutes then came out to take me back to one of the interrogation rooms. I gave Crutch what was left of my Cruller and the three of us followed OJ back for the interview.

"You can't bring your mutt back here," he began. Crutch growled and I turned back again toward the front desk. Crutch might like another donut although we would need a workout after this carb load.

"Jesus Finn, come back here, he can stay," he said sounding tired and exasperated. *Just where I like him.*

Another about face and we all took seats in the interview room.

"Okay Finn, I just need you to lay out in your own words what the fuck happened this morning. I have three bodies in the morgue and two more in the hospital with bullet wounds. Based on the last forty-eight hours we have four bodies, five if you count the girl and you are the prime suspect in two of them and the common denominator in all four."

I didn't respond.

"Look you are looking like a one-man wrecking crew so tell me what happened this morning."

For the next ten minutes, I outlined what had happened at the boatyard. My going to search the boat for any evidence regarding what had happened to Nieve, my link through her cousin Annalee and the fact that the *Kilimanjaro* had rammed the boat of my partner.

I covered my being asked to look into it by my boss who represented the insurance company for *Blue Agave* but I left out the connection with Hank and the notebook. I figured OJ didn't need to know that little detail.

"Why did you go to the boatyard with three armed security personnel?" he asked.

"OJ, I'd been attacked twice in the last forty-eight hours by guys with guns. I figured I'd better even the odds."

"Who are these guys that seem to be after you?" he asked. "It feels like we are suddenly in the middle of a war with mercenaries, RPG's, M4's and snipers."

It must have been the use of the word 'war' that triggered something in me. Was this some kind of war?

"Look OJ, none of this makes any sense to me. I've been beaten up, shot with an RPG, burned and knocked unconscious. I'm tired and hungry in spite of the donuts."

"Do you need us or can we go?" Stacy chimed in. "My client has been open, forthcoming and answered all your questions."

We waited for his answer.

Finally, all OJ said was, "Go." I actually felt sorry for him.

"Stacy, I need to get some rest so let's go back to Shark Key, check in on Annalee and get the notebook to Hank. I want to learn more about what he knows that might explain this 'war' we are in."

After a quick stop at the bank to get the notebook, we headed back up the Keys and were pulling into Shark Key when my phone rang.

"Finn, it's Abacus." He sounded strange.

CHAPTER TWELVE

Oh, shit. I meant to call him about potential visitors from Blunt Force who Digger had mentioned.

Trying to sound casual I asked, "What's up?"

"Mr. Pilar," said a voice I didn't recognize, "You have a very nice little bar here."

"Thank you," was all I could think of to say.

"Mr. Pilar, your partner here has been telling me all about it."

"I appreciate that you keep calling me Mr. Pilar, but in my experience the only people who call me that turn out to be assholes or collection agents. Which one are you?"

He chuckled. *Not a good sign.*

"Mr. Pilar, you have something that belongs to us so I guess you could call us collection agents, here to collect."

"Well, as you put it so nicely, I will give you the address of my business manager and you can call him to collect." I hung up because they always call back.

"Who was that?" asked Stacy.

"It seems somebody thinks I have something of theirs and they are visiting Abacus to collect it."

"Damn Finn, this is getting serious. What the hell is in this notebook?"

"I will wait for them to call back." The phone rang again. I let it ring until it stopped.

"Aren't you going to answer it? Stacy asked. "Abacus could be in trouble."

A voicemail popped up on the screen. I opened it up and listened to Abacus shouting "NO! NO!" then a gunshot and a scream. The message ended.

"Motherfucker!" I screamed at the phone while pounding the steering wheel.

"Finn?" cried Stacy but I already had the Mustang in reverse, I did a one-eighty-degree spin and tore out of the entrance to Shark Key. I was at least twenty minutes out so I called 911 to report shots fired at *Mockingbird* and accelerated down U.S. 1 doing over ninety.

We sped across Boca Chica, and Stock Island then down Flagler Ave. I was screaming to a stop outside the *Mockingbird* in twelve minutes with two of Key West's finest on my tail.

I figured what the hell was a couple of speeding tickets when I was already potentially facing three murder charges.

The ambulance was already there and I raced into the bar to see Abacus sitting on a stool at the bar. The EMTs were working on his hand.

The cops that had been racing to catch me as we sped down Flagler at almost one hundred miles per hour came barging in with guns drawn. The first through the door was good old Officer *Friendless* screaming, "Down on the floor asshole!"

Just my luck to get this guy on the case.

I walked up to Abacus who smiled with a grimace. "I'm beginning to rethink our partnership, Finn. You seem to have a very nasty habit of attracting some nasty friends."

"You know what they say Abacus. Keep your friends close and your enemies closer."

"Did you get that from a fortune cookie?" he quipped.

The Taser hit me in the back and I collapsed in

agony on the bar floor. I made a mental note to get the floor cleaned when this was all over.

I had forgotten all about Officer *Friendless* who it seemed continued to feel I was in need of being subdued as a dangerous felon.

As I writhed on the ground, Stacy stepped in and shouted, "Officer! Stop!" whereupon Crutch began to growl and seemed ready to leap to her defense.

Oh yeah, protect her. I'm the one who feeds and walks you most of the time. What about me? I didn't want to have to get him rescued from Doggy Jail for the second time in one day so I commanded, "Crutch, sit," which must have come out as, "Cruft, spit," because he was in mid-leap at *Friendless* when *Abacus* grabbed his collar with his good hand. *Ah, the joys of Taser exposure.*

Friendless grabbed my arms and the next thing I knew my hands were zip-cuffed behind my back.

"Officer, please release Mr. Pilar," came a voice out of my line of sight. Then OJ appeared. "Jesus Finn, can't I leave you alone for an hour without you getting arrested?" he asked as he cut the cuffs off me with the Benchmade Tactical knife my ex-wife had given him when we had become partners many years ago. *It's a long story.*

"I just missed your rapier wit and our scintillating conversations," I remarked, thanking him for the hand to steady me as I stood up. I only hope I will someday have the chance to be on the other end of a Taser with Officer Friendless.

"Finn, I am beginning to think I should lock you up for your own safety." He began, "So what's the story this time?"

"Abacus," I suggested, "Maybe you can tell this one. I think he is tired of hearing my voice."

"Well, let me think," he paused then reached for a

bottle of *Herradura* Anejo and two glasses. He poured two fingers in each and handed me one.

"About two this afternoon after the noon crowd had died down three guys came in and sat at the bar. They said they had heard that Finn was the owner of the bar and that they were old buddies from his Navy days. One was older than the other two but all three were clearly fit although rough around the edges."

"They asked if I had your number and could I call you for them. I placed the call and the young guys grabbed me while the older one took the phone."

I stepped in to pick up the story, "The voice on the phone said that I had something that was theirs and they wanted it back. I offered that I had no idea what they were talking about, called them assholes and hung up."

Abacus jumped back in, "They tried again to call 'hero boy' here and he didn't answer so they dragged me over to the bar. One pulled out a gun while the other locked the door of the bar. They called Finn again then pointed the gun at me. I shouted, "Don't do it or something like that, then they fired the gun into the floor and one of the young guys broke my finger by smashing it with the butt of the gun."

I thanked them for coming into the bar and told them that Finn would get back to them. No, actually I recall screaming in pain, telling them to fuck off and die or words to that effect. That must have been when he knocked me out, stole a bottle of our best Tequila on display and took off.

I turned to OJ and said, "Dude, it's a small island, can you set up a BOLO on these guys and try to track them down?"

"First things first, Finn. Abacus can you describe these perps well enough for a sketch artist?" he asked.

"I can do you one better. We have cameras in the

office to deal with problems in the bar. I'll get you the tapes." He went to the office then returned a few minutes later empty handed and looking dejected.

"I guess they took the discs with them after they knocked me out."

"Thanks anyway Abacus. I will get an artist down here to take your descriptions and will put out a 'Be On the Look Out' for them."

Turning to me he asked, "Finn, might you have something they're looking for?"

I always try to answer an uncomfortable question with a question. "Abacus, did they give you any hint about that they were looking for?"

He scratched his head and said, "They didn't say what it was but they sure thought that you were the one who knew what it would be and where it was."

"OJ, I wonder if these were the same guys who were at the boatyard the other night and again this morning. They seemed to be looking for something then as well." Again duck the question. I continued, "I know one thing for sure though. I don't have anything they're looking for unless it's my good looks, boyish charm and great sense of humor."

Stacy chuckled, and OJ just shook his head.

I decided to throw him a bone. "One thing I just remembered OJ. I was at the morgue this morning to have Annalee identify the body of her cousin who was the girl killed on the boat. Digger mentioned that two guys had visited the morgue earlier and asked to see the bodies of the guys who were killed at the boatyard. Then they asked if he knew where I could be found. He told them at the *Mockingbird*."

"Damn, Finn you could have warned me," whined Abacus.

"Yeah, you're right Abacus. I'm sorry but I guess getting into a gun fight, being blown up by an RPG, burned and then tortured by the police as a potential suspect in three murders all in the last twelve hours put me off my game," I tossed off sarcastically.

"Tortured by the police," laughed OJ. "Yeah, donuts and coffee could be seen as torture by a diabetic, but wait," he paused, "You're the one who brought the donuts."

"Well if you had tasted the coffee you'd know it's torture," I added.

"Enough you two!" cried Stacy, "If you can stop swinging your dicks around for a minute, we might be able to figure out what the fuck is going on."

She made a good point.

"OJ, if you can get a decent artist sketch from Abacus, you can check with Digger to see if it's the same guys."

"Stacy, you and I should go back to Hank's place and try to learn more about this charter."

That seemed to represent a plan so we headed out, with only Officer Friendless looking pissed that he did not get to arrest me. I waved at him then flipped him the bird. *I'm really good at making friends.*

~ ~ ~

We hopped in the Mustang with Crutch in the back seat and drove back to Shark Key. We called ahead to my favorite Italian spot on Stock Island, *Roostica* to order pizzas for the gang at Hank's place then stopped to pick them up.

With six Extra Large Red Pizzas and four extra Large White pizzas, including my favorite Cuban Mix, we held a brief wake for the WWF operator who was killed at the boatyard that morning. We drank a toast to his sacrifice and ate the pizza while his team told stories of his exploits in Iraq and Afghanistan.

Once we finished dinner, I kicked off the discussion that included Hank, Dale from WWF, Matt, Stacy, and Annalee.

"Let me do a quick recap of what we know," I

began. "This all started for most of us with the arrival of the *Kilimanjaro* crashing into Abacus's boat. He found Annalee's cousin, Nieve, sadly deceased on board. Hank revealed that he had chartered the *Kilimanjaro* to bring a secret notebook to the U.S. Since we retrieved the notebook, we have since been shot at, blown up and blackmailed to give it to what appears to be a group of mercenaries working for Blunt Force. The motive in all this seems to be possession of the notebook. Have I missed anything?"

The group murmured, looked at each other shaking their heads like dashboard hula dolls and all I got was crickets.

"Okay so Hank, we have all been chasing this notebook. What the fuck is in it that is worth all this drama?"

All eyes turned to Hank.

CHAPTER THIRTEEN

Oddly, he suddenly seemed to have the look of a deer caught in the headlights of an oncoming freight train. He appeared to collect himself and began, "Grab a beer as this will take a while."

"Just give it to us," insisted Matt. "Quit dancing around."

"All right. I don't have an answer for whom, but as for motive, the bottom line is that buried in the notebook in code, is a formula for an enzyme-based process that will accelerate the breakdown of hemp waste. It enables us to produce a high octane fuel at a fraction of the price of traditional methods."

He stopped and seemed to expect us to gasp with astonishment. When it didn't happen, he exclaimed, "Don't you get it? This could signal the end of all petroleum-based fuels; oil, natural gas, and coal!"

When we all looked at him like he was a member of the tin foil hat crowd, he said with some exasperation, "Here's the net-net. Global annual oil production is approximately thirty-five billion barrels; that's billion with a capital B. At fifty bucks a barrel, that is over one point five trillion dollars a year. Is that enough motive for you?"

Suddenly the room took on a distinct chill. Billions were bad enough but trillions were nuts.

In an attempt to inject some oxygen into the room

after he had sucked most of it out, I jumped in, "So what are you saying, this formula can destroy the oil industry and save the planet?"

It sounded crazy when I said it but all eyes turned to Hank as he responded. "Yes, the only outcome big oil is interested in is either owning it, to bury it or if necessary, destroying it so it won't become available and kill the one point five trillion a year gravy train."

I don't think any of us could really take it in.

Hank continued, "Over one-third of global production is controlled by seven of the world's most unstable countries including Russia, Iran, Iraq, and Venezuela. These countries are completely dependent on oil to support their populations. If this formula becomes available, the global economy shifts and the resulting turmoil could be catastrophic."

No one else seemed to be able to take a breath so I threw out, "Hank, while I'm interested in how all this came about, it's probably not going to help at this point. What did you have in mind when you brought this over from Cuba rather than just leaving well enough alone?"

He took a deep breath and went for broke. "Finn, you know I have spent millions developing a hemp fiber-based car and now an offshore racing boat."

I hadn't realized it was millions, but his choice.

"My goal is to showcase hemp as the global solution for transitioning to carbon negative, climate positive resources. Hemp can eliminate resource blackmail by oil producers, promote climate recovery and put developing nations on an equal footing with the wealthy nations which currently have an energy advantage."

He looked around the room. "I need your help to protect this formula until I can prove the value of hemp."

Hank had become incredibly animated as he

amped up about his vision. His eyes took on the gleam that I imagined would be familiar to people under the spell of Rasputin, Jim Jones, or any number of other religious fanatics or demagogues.

Matt, ever the pragmatist took over. "Hank in the SEALs, the next question would be, what's the plan?"

"If by that you mean what am I planning, then the net of it is I'm planning to enter my hemp racing boat in the upcoming World Championship Ocean Racing event here in Key West using a hemp body and the biofuel made from this formula. I want to showcase the fact that we will beat all the petroleum-based competition. The publicity should help protect the formula and launch a revolution in global energy production and manufacturing."

"Imagine the impact on carbon emissions if we could grow hemp on islands like Hawaii, then use it to build cars and create a locally sourced biofuel rather than importing oil at a huge cost."

He was starting to ramp up again so I shut it down.

"Hank, I need to digest all this and better understand your objectives. I for one am going to crash now and tackle this in the morning. I suggest as a first step we all get some rest."

Matt took charge of the protection details and shift assignments and I stumbled upstairs with Stacy as my mind swirled trying to get my arms around the magnitude of what Hank was trying to accomplish.

After a quick shower that revived my spirits and rekindled my curiosity regarding Stacy's interest in chocolate, I reached over to give her a gentle nudge.

"Finn, do you ever think with your big head?" and she giggled.

"I *am* thinking with the big head," I chuckled looking down. "This is my big head."

Stacy paused and in her best imitation of a

southern belle said, "Why sa, I do declaire," as she looked down, then fanning herself added, "I do believe you are causin' me to blush."

She leaned over and smiled.

Taking the bottle of Kahlua, she took a generous slug then took me into her mouth still dripping with the residue of the sweet chocolate alcohol that caused a very slight burning of the tip of my now fully distended cock.

I took the bottle from her taking a small sip as she climbed on top of me. I began to lick her inner thigh then the entrance to her now equally engorged honey pot.

We licked, sipped, and sucked until we could bear it no longer.

She began to writhe as I clung to her ass forcing my tongue deeper into her as she came, again and again, covering my face with a glaze of sweet orgasmic honey.

As she came, she took me deeper and deeper into her mouth until she was practically swallowing me. I could feel her throat convulsing on the tip of my penis as I exploded.

We collapsed and in an exhausted stupor fell asleep in each other's arms as Crutch guarded the door looking frustrated. I need to get him laid I thought as I drifted off into oblivion.

~ ~ ~

I awoke to the smell of bacon and coffee drifting up from the kitchen. I lay in bed savoring the memory of last night with Stacy and feeling myself beginning to recover. I reached over to caress her bare breast when she mumbled, "You need to feed me first then we can talk."

I looked down and said to my now receding erection, "You'll have to wait, dude. Got to feed the little lady first but hold that thought."

I threw on my jeans and a tee shirt and offered to get Stacy coffee in bed. She mumbled something and rolled over revealing a perfect ass peeking out from under the loose sheet.

As chubby returned, I looked down, "I told you to hold on to that thought dude."

Downstairs Matt was in the kitchen chatting with Consuelo as she cooked up breakfast. He glanced over as I came in and he smiled. "Get a good night sleep?"

"Yes thank you," I responded. "Did I miss anything?"

"No," he replied "but clearly *we* did. Next time you might want to check the mirror before you join us for breakfast."

When my quizzical look gave away my confusion he added, "If I stuck a piece of bacon in your mouth you'd look like one of those Glazed Maple Bacon donuts from the Glazed Donut shop on Eaton.

As the toaster popped up a couple of slices, Consuelo chuckled, "Not the only thing popping up I imagine."

With witty repartee confirming my diminished state I offered, "You can both go fuck yourselves." I retreated to their burst of laughter.

With that, I took the coffee up to Stacy then hopped into the shower. By the time I got out, the bed was empty, the coffee gone and Stacy in the final stages of dressing. The look on my freshly scrubbed face must have given away my disappointment.

She said, "Time to get to work, *big guy*. We need to eat, then make a plan." With that, she gave me a chaste peck on the cheek, gently grabbed my crotch and added, "Until later, dude." She headed down for breakfast. *This girl is a keeper.*

Matt and Hank were already deep in discussion when we came into the kitchen. Consuelo came over with two plates of eggs with bacon and home fries then joined us. Matt took the lead and said, "If you two are up to it . . . " he paused.

When we ignored him he began again.

"Hank and I have been discussing next steps."

"Basically nothing has changed in his mind. The races begin in two weeks and the boat is entered in the Unlimited class. Between now and then we need to get the drivers and pit crew together, decode the formula for making the fuel then make enough fuel to power the boat. We also need to protect the boat between now and the start of the races. Finally, we need to track down the people who killed Nieve and who have threatened us assuming they are the same people. Did I miss anything?"

As we looked around at each other, I added, "Let's not forget to make sure we all survive this thing in one piece." ??

"Right." Matt continued, "Hank you are the one who knows this notebook and potentially how to decode it. You work with Stacy and Hector our security guy to figure that part out. Okay?"

"Got it," was all Hank said.

"Finn you work with Dale to find drivers and crew and track down who is trying to kill us." We both nodded.

"I will work with Annalee and Consuelo to protect the boat and make the fuel once Hank gets the formula worked out." Consuelo nodded in agreement.

"I will keep six of the guards from WWF on site. The other two teams will take three guards each for twenty-four/seven personal security. Any questions?"

We all looked around at each other. "Nothing? Okay, let's do a call-in every four hours and meet back here at eighteen hundred hours for a debrief.

With that Dale and I headed out in the Mustang

toward Lower Keys Medical. I had an idea where I might start to find crew for the boat. Then I wanted to see if we could set up a sting for the Blunt Force guys.

I call ahead to see if Digger was around and found out he had the day off so I knew he could be found at Harpoon Harry's having breakfast with GG. I tried his cell and he picked up after a couple of rings.

"Finn, anybody but you would be leaving me a voicemail. What's up?"

"Hey Digger, how are the corn beef hash and poached eggs?" I asked.

"I know, I'm really boring and predictable but for seven bucks it's the best breakfast in town."

"Listen I need some help so I will be there in about ten minutes."

"Do you want me to order anything for you?" he asked.

"No, we just ate thanks. See you in ten," and I hung up.

My next call was to my old friend and business partner Ricardo Ramos. Ricardo owns a large hacienda in Mexico's agave region near Guadalajara. He is also an investor in the *Mockingbird* bar that Abacus and I own. When we opened the bar, he agreed to supply us with very special tequila from his family's private stock that we exclusively feature at the *Mockingbird*.

We first met when he needed a local security contact in Key West so I became his local liaison with the Key West Police Department. Ricardo was in town as a sponsor of the Super Boat Unlimited class catamaran *Agave Thunder* that was competing in the Annual Super Boat World Championships.

My call was routed to his office and they told me he was visiting the Guadalupe Valley near Rosarito just south of the San Diego-Tijuana border.

"Can you please have him call me? It's urgent."

"Of course Senor Finn. Is this the best number?" she asked.

"Si, muchas gracias," I replied in my best Spanish.

The three of us plus Crutch continued down North Roosevelt to Palm Avenue across to Eaton, and down Margaret to Harry's on Caroline. Crutch got excited as we pulled up thinking it was bacon time.

Digger was sitting at his usual table out front with a satiated look on his face and an empty plate on the table. Debbie our favorite server saw us arrive and she came over with coffee as the three of us pulled chairs over to join Digger and GG. She already had two strips of bacon for Crutch. *I never got service that fast.*

"Digger, I need your help," I began after introductions.

I brought him up to speed.

"So what can I do?" he asked.

"I am trying to track down some of the guys from the Marine Force Recon team you worked on in Iraq. Do any of those guys owe you a favor that we might leverage to learn more about the Blunt Force contractors who ended up in your morgue?"

He thought for a minute then offered, "Let me make a few calls and get back to you. I assume it's urgent as always?"

"Digger, we have less than two weeks to finish Hank's boat and run trials to get it set up for the Super Boat World Championships. In the meantime, we need to figure out who killed Nieve and then tried to kill me. Urgent doesn't begin to cover it."

GG cut in and said, "You may have less time than you think. The Tropical Depression that was hovering off Jamaica was upgraded to a Tropical Storm. Now named Margaret, the storm has sustained winds of seventy miles per hour and is moving west at ten."

"What are you saying?" I asked with an edge in my voice.

"Well you know fisherman, we don't give a shit

until the winds really start to howl but this one seems to have a few people spooked. The radio chatter is that it could follow a similar path to Hurricane Wilma back in 2005 and a slight shift further west could take her directly over Havana. That would put Key West in the bullseye."

Shit, that's all we need I thought.

CHAPTER FOURTEEN

Key West is rather uniquely situated in proximity to Cuba. Cuba's mountains provide some protection from the full force of hurricanes coming up from the south, as the mountains tend to break up the integrity of a storm. Although the warm waters of the Florida Straits can help it reform, it only has a few hours over the Strait so it is usually weaker should it hit Key West.

The last serious hurricane to impact Key West was Wilma, a Category 3 hurricane with sustained winds of more than one hundred and ten miles per hour. She also had the lowest ever recorded pressure in the Atlantic basin and caused almost thirty billion dollars in damage in total. The damage in Key West was primarily due to the storm surge. As much as six feet of water was recorded in low-lying sections of the island.

I usually relied on the fisherman more than NOAA and if GG was even mildly concerned, then we needed to prepare for the worst.

My cell rang and it was Ricardo.

"Hola, mi amigo. Que pasa?"

"Finn, my friend, you called and I will help with whatever you need."

"Ricardo, your office said you are in the Guadeloupe Valley. Are you looking to get into the wine business now?" I asked.

"No my friend, if I was looking to make wine, I

would add to my new place in Napa. I recently bought a small family winery near Saint Helena. I loved the property and we make about a thousand cases a year. I will send you one."

"Ricardo you are too kind. You know Stacy loves good wine."

"How is the beautiful Stacy? If you ever decide to get married, Isabella and I could host you at the Hacienda. But enough about the family. What is so urgent?" he asked.

"Ricardo my friend, I have a huge favor to ask," I began. "I am looking for a crew to run a boat in the Unlimited Super Boat race in Key West. I know you race in it and thought you might know a crew looking for a ride."

The phone went quiet then he said, "I don't know if you heard but we had to pull out of the race last week. The boat was totaled on its way to Florida when the trailer jackknifed in the mountains in North Carolina."

"Oh Ricardo, I am so sorry. I know how much you loved that boat. Can it be repaired?"

"Well maybe but not in time for this year's race. What is this boat you have?" Clearly, his curiosity was piqued.

For the next ten minutes, I outlined the situation and in the end, he said, "I love it. I'm in. Maybe we can have it sponsored by *Tequila Mockingbird* and we can drive traffic to the bar."

"Ricardo this boat and its owner are in the line of fire of some nasty people, probably connected to big oil. I want to make sure both you and the crew understand the risks."

He laughed. "Finn my friend, these guys race unlimited class super boats at average speeds of a hundred and seventy miles an hour on a course where wind and waves change every second. It's like being in a thousand car crashes in an hour to drive these things. Risks are what they live for so don't worry about them. In fact, this will just make it all the more exciting."

"Okay, I have an idea. How quickly can you get here with your boat? And can you send me a picture of it?"

We wrapped up the call agreeing that he and his crew would be in Key West in two days but they would come to Shark Key first. In the meantime, we needed to get the biofuel process underway and figure out who was after us while keeping an eye on the weather.

No pressure.

I decided to call Hank to give him an update. Stacy picked up.

"Hey handsome, how's my favorite boy toy," she asked.

.   "Played out at the moment but looking forward to our next play date," I replied with none to subtle lust in my voice.

"Put it away big boy. You have work to do."

"Where's Hank?" I asked.

"We are at the bank and he's in the manager's office scanning a copy of the notebook. I recommended that we keep the original locked in the safe deposit box in the event that we ever need to prove origin for patent purposes."

"Got it. Good thinking," I offered. "What's next?"

"We're going to head back to the house and try to figure out the formula which seems to be in code."

"Okay, well tell Hank we have a crew for the boat and they will be here in two days. Ricardo came through and has offered to give us his crew for this race."

"I thought he was running his own boat in this race like he does every year," Stacy replied.

I gave her the background and she said in her usual pragmatic fashion, "Too bad for him, but good for us."

"Listen, I just had a thought," I mused. "I am not far

from you so we will come over to the bank and meet you. "There has been a lot of interest in the notebook and if we are moving it around, I think we need more security. We can drive back to the house together."

"Finn, we will be fine. We have Hector and the original notebook is still in the bank." She said sounding a little miffed.

"Stacy, I have an idea and will be over in five minutes to join you." I hung up.

We got to the bank just as Hank was finishing up the copying in the manager's office.

"Hank," I said, "I'm a little concerned that when we are outside the bank we are vulnerable to Blunt Force trying to steal the notebook," I explained my next idea.

I talked to the bank manager and she gave me three manila envelopes. Inside each, I put a blank thumb drive with the words *Notebook Copy* written in large letters on the envelope. I gave Stacy one with instructions to go with Hector and my guard to Shark Key. I then gave Hank a copy and told him to go with Dale back to the house. I took the third envelope.

After giving each team instructions, I held back. I went next door to get one of my favorite snacks at Cuzzy Bubbaz, a hole in the wall on Southard serving amazing Dagwood sandwiches and shrimp and lobster tacos. I sat in the window as the others left and ordered the Lobster Poutine – meaty fries smothered in white gravy with huge chunks of fresh lobster. I'm going to need at least a half hour of swimming to get rid of these calories but somebody had to take one for the team.

Both the other teams drove down Southard, which is a one-way street. I watched to see if anyone started to follow either team. I told them to drive past Duval over to Whitehead then turn at the Green Parrot with one team going left toward Truman and the other right toward Eaton. I didn't see anyone following either team so after finishing the Poutine, Crutch and I headed out on our own back to the house.

The idea was taken from a page from the street hustle *Three Card Monte* in which only one of the three cards is the Ace. In this case, *I* was the Ace.

To make sure Stacy was protected and Hank was covered as well, I would be the easy mark. Using this old trick, I hoped to get Blunt Force to reveal themselves as they searched for the notebook and the formula.

Crutch and I hopped in the Mustang and drove down to Duval then all the way down to South Street turning left toward the airport. As I drove up South Street I came up behind a slow-moving panel van. As we stopped at the new stop sign at Reynolds, a black SUV ran into the back of me, driving me into the panel truck.

Knowing this was a carjacking seemed obvious but doing anything about it was impossible. Heroically I put my hands on my head and Crutch covered his eyes with his paws in the front floor well. The back window of the van opened and the barrel of a rifle became visible pointed at my head.

A man I did not recognize got out of the passenger side of the SUV, walked up beside the Mustang and asked, "Are you okay?" as he reached into the Mustang and picked up the brown manila envelope with the thumb drive in it. *I need to remember to not get a convertible next time.*

Once he had the envelope, he offered to call the police and walked back to the SUV at the same time puncturing the Mustang's rear tire sidewall. To the casual observer, it would look like a minor fender bender that was resolved without incident. In seconds he was gone, taking Reynolds toward Casa Marina with the panel van right behind him.

I only hoped that the GPS software loaded onto each of the thumb drives would lead us to where Blunt

Force was based. I called Matt to give him an update and he began to track the thumb drive.

It was about time we took the fight to the enemy rather than always being on the defensive. In combat, if you stop moving you die. Winning is about putting pressure on the other side. By the time I got back to the house everyone had made it back safely and we needed to debrief.

As I had hoped, the others had uneventful trips so I explained what had happened to me.

"Wait a minute, you put us out as bait for these assholes?" asked Stacy. "What the fuck were you thinking? We could have been killed. I could have been killed." She was pissed again.

"Babe, listen, I put you with two of Dale's best guys and Hank was with Dale. I played the odds that they would go after the easiest target. Me."

"Well next time Finn, if you are going to play the odds with my life let me know in advance," and she stormed out of the room. *Damn, there go my evening plans.*

Crutch growled at me, turned and went after her.

"Anybody else?" I said to the rest of the room.

Just at that point, Annalee rushed into the room and said, "Finn, you need to see this!" and she headed back into the kitchen.

"Great now what?" I mumbled as I followed her. I have to admit that she was not bad to watch from behind. *Behave yourself, Finnigan, I thought.*

In the kitchen, she pointed to the TV tuned to the Weather Channel. The announcer, Jim Cantore, was standing on a beach with wind tearing at his nylon jacket.

"Tropical Storm Margaret has just been declared a Category 1 hurricane with sustained winds of eighty-two miles per hour. Currently, it is just off the west coast of Jamaica moving northwest in the Caribbean Sea. The Doppler radar has it tracking toward the Yucatan Peninsula.

This is a very slow moving storm so it is growing in strength with each hour. It is forecast to approach the Cayman Islands in the next twelve hours and could be a Category 2 at that time. We will keep you posted every hour but if you are in the path of the storm, now is the time to prepare."

Annalee said, "Finn, I need to head back to Cuba. My family is in Holguin but my brother is in Havana and I need to be there for him."

What could I say but, "Of course, I understand, what can I do to help?"

She leaned over and kissed me. "You have been so sweet, can you just make sure that when this is all over that we can have Nieve's body sent back to Cuba?"

My now semi aroused self, wanted to say, "Can you stay a little while longer?" My better angels responded, "Of course. When is your flight?"

"There is a flight out of Miami tonight at seven so I should be able to make it up there by then." With those big beautiful eyes beseeching me she continued, "Finn, you have been a good friend and I will always remember your kindness. If you are ever again in Cuba, be sure to find me."

She began to give me a chaste peck on the cheek but I couldn't resist turning into it. Her lips were soft and her tongue gently searched for mine then she pulled back. "Perhaps another time," was all she said, then turned and left the room.

How about tonight? As I turned to watch her go, I saw Stacy standing in the doorway to the living room with a tear running down her cheek.

Oh shit. Stacy ran from the room.

"Stacy, wait!" I called out just as Matt burst out with, "Now we've got him!"

As I ran into the living room after Stacy I stopped short. Matt was hunched over a computer. "Finn, we got them. They are holed up in a couple of storage lockers on Catherine Street. They probably have a rental nearby."

I heard the Mustang fire up and the tires spray gravel as it took off out of the driveway. I had used the spare to fix the punctured tire so she better not get another flat. Damn, where would she go? I ignored Matt and called her cell only to get voicemail.

"Stacy, babe, please Annalee was just saying goodbye. She is going back to Cuba because of the storm. It was no big deal. Come on babe, she's just a friend."

"Your time is up," announced the voicemail message. *Shit*

I called back. "Stace, come on. Please call me back so I can explain."

Clearly, at this point, she was not going to pick up. Damn, I am really bad at this relationship stuff. You would think I would have learned by now.

Matt dragged me back with, "Dude, she'll get over whatever stupid thing you did. You need to focus on dealing with Blunt Force if we are going to figure out who killed Nieve and help Hank with this race."

"This from the guy who's been divorced three times," I replied sarcastically.

"Learn from my mistakes," he responded. "Give her time. You can't fix stupid and I assume you did something stupid so let her cool down. Now let me know when your head is back in the game."

He called Dale in from outside where he was setting up the perimeter and assignments for the night. With the notebook having been emailed from the bank and Hank working on decoding it, we needed to make sure the boat was protected.

We spent the next thirty minutes developing a plan that would help us accomplish the defensive moves then we began on the offense ones.

It was clear that Blunt Force was ready to kill to either get the formula or absent that, destroy it. We needed to take the fight to them to knock them off center.

"Matt, assuming Blunt Force is working for someone on contract, how do we figure out who they are working for?"

"Isn't it obvious?" said Hank as he walked in our conversation. "You follow the money. Dupree Petroleum has billions if not trillions of motives."

I had to jump in, "Hank I have been thinking about this and while that's true, the most obvious villain being Dupree Petroleum, can you think of any others?"

"Like who?" he asked.

"Let's assume that Dupree is one, but what about others who stand to benefit if oil remains the dominant fuel source for the foreseeable future? How about drilling companies, oil-producing nations dependent on oil revenues, oil based chemical companies, to name just a few. I mean even environmental groups could be trying to protect donor revenue sources. They are all dependent on oil for a living."

Not wanting to leave any stone unturned, I offered, "Even our own government may be involved. Imagine the costs to convert all of our military hardware to burn biofuel. Even small equipment modifications would cost billions when you scale it up."

"Finn, what's your point?" asked Matt.

"I am not sure we are asking the right question."

"What are you thinking?" Matt shot back impatiently.

"I don't know exactly but what if this is all a red herring, a distraction to take our focus off some other objective?"

I paused then began again. "This whole thing got

started with a girl found dead on a boat that drifted into Abacus' boat in the harbor. What if it was driven into his boat intentionally? From the beginning they had me involved, first because of the boat being rammed then because of the girl with the tattoo that I would recognize. They went to a lot of trouble to get her on the boat. Why might somebody want me involved?"

Now I had their attention.

"Let's go back to the basic motives for any crime: love, lust, lucre, and loathing. Could it be that someone is coming after me for one of these motives or more likely they are using me to accomplish one or more of them?"

Hank jumped in with, "Look, don't make this more complicated than it needs to be. My family won't like me getting in the way of their business by using an old family formula to do it".

"I retrieved the notebook and chartered a boat to get it to the States. They found out somehow and took control of the crew. Maybe the girl on the boat was a spy for them and after getting rid of the Capitan and first mate, they killed Nieve. When they couldn't find the notebook, they drifted the boat into Key West then they planned to steal it from me once I retrieved it."

"Okay," I acknowledged. "Then why get a girl I would recognize to be their spy?"

Matt stepped in and suggested, "We don't have enough information at this point so we need to make an effort to learn more from Blunt Force. By now they must realize that the thumb drive did not contain the notebook copy so they will be looking for another way to get it."

My cell rang and an unknown number showed on the screen.

"Hello," I answered.

"Finn, it's Annalee." Then a different voice came on the line.

"Pilar, you are a very difficult man."

CHAPTER FIFTEEN

"Who is this? I asked.

"My name's not important. What's important is that your friend here is a guest of ours and we will be entertaining her until you give us what belongs to us."

"And what might that be?" I asked knowing exactly what they wanted.

"Pilar, you have a notebook that belongs to us and we would like it back. You have one hour to bring it to us or the girl dies. You know we mean business because of what happened to her cousin. I will call with instructions in thirty minutes."

"Wait, you already took it from me a few hours ago. I don't have it." I lied.

"We both know the thumb drive was blank, so last chance, bring the notebook to us or the girl dies." He hung up.

"Shit!" I exclaimed. "Some asshole has taken Annalee and is threatening to kill her if I don't get the notebook to him in an hour. It has to be Blunt Force assuming they are the ones who took the thumb drive from me today. And I for one am tired of these guys putting constant pressure on us. We need to put it on them for a change."

I put myself in charge. "Matt, I need you to stay here and with three guys protect the boat. Hank, where are we with the fuel formula?"

Hank thought for a moment then said, "My guesstimate is I need another two hours to test the last batch to see if I have the octane levels that meet the standards, then we are good to go."

I hesitated then asked, "If we give them the notebook, will they be able to duplicate it?"

Slowly Hank said, "It is possible with enough time, but we should have enough of a lead to demonstrate that this biofuel is effective and can be produced in sufficient volume to be competitive with petroleum-based fuels."

I needed time to think. I'm not sure how long I stood at the window looking out at the ocean. I was broken out of my reverie by my cell phone ringing. I picked it up and hit answer. It is a smartphone after all.

"Pilar, you have thirty minutes to meet us with the original notebook or the girl dies."

"Fuck you!" I replied and hit 'end call'. I really don't like people telling me what to do.

Two minutes later I got a text. It was a picture of Annalee standing in front of a hooded man who was holding a knife to her throat.

The phone rang again. I hit answer.

"The next picture will be her wearing what her cousin had on her throat. Now do I have your attention?"

"All right, where and when?" I inquired.

"You will buy one ticket on the sailboat *Danger* for their sunset cruise. You will come alone. You will put the notebook in a double zip lock bag and take it with you. You will get further instructions once you are on board and underway." He hung up.

I briefed everyone on the instructions then headed out. I already felt in some way responsible for Nieve and did not want to also have Annalee's death on my conscience as well.

~ ~ ~

Danger Charters is one of a small fleet of old coastal schooners that are used to take tourists on a variety of sunset and private charters off the coast of Key West. They generally leave out of the harbor marina off the Margaritaville Resort on Front Street.

After getting the original notebook from the bank, I was just able to catch the six-thirty sunset cruise. There were about fifteen people on board and the wine started to flow as we left the mouth of the harbor.

After exiting the harbor, the sails went up and a fresh breeze was taking us out toward the mangrove islands on the near horizon off the coast of Key West. My phone rang.

"In exactly twenty minutes, you will throw the notebook sealed in the bag overboard," demanded the now familiar voice.

"Not before I see the girl is alive and well asshole," I replied.

He hung up.

I waited.

Just before the twenty minutes was up, a boat suddenly appeared from behind the island we were approaching. It was a thirty or so foot long go-fast boat with four outboards so a capability of upwards of sixty miles per hour. It headed toward us and as it passed within about twenty yards of our stern, suddenly Annalee appeared on deck from the cabin below. She was gagged with her hands tied behind her back.

My phone rang.

"Toss the bag off the starboard side then I'll release the girl," he instructed.

"Fuck you asshole. Not until you release the girl," I commanded.

At that point, he shoved her over the side into the water.

I was now faced with three choices: I could dive

into the water to save her and take the book with me; I could toss the book over the side for them to pick it up; or I could toss it onto the boat, then go after it.

The crew and tourists had no idea what was going on but saw that a girl was now in the water struggling to stay afloat. Trying ever to be the hero, I dove in with the notebook.

The speedboat proceeded to position itself between me and Annalee.

A man on board the speedboat yelled, "The notebook or the girl, Pilar. You choose!"

I tossed the notebook toward the boat and he reached down with a fishing net to pick it up.

"You've got the book now, so MOVE!" I shouted starting to hyperventilate to make the dive under his boat.

He revved the engines and within seconds was on plane headed for the mangrove island from which he had come minutes before. I searched in his wake for any sign of Annalee.

I dove down into the crystal clear water and was able to see her struggling just below the surface to stay afloat. She was kicking with her legs but I could see they were tied and she was in a state of panic.

My mind flashed back to the second phase in BUD/S during my Navy SEAL training. We would have our hands and feet tied and had to swim fifty yards in the frigid waters of the pool. The feeling of helplessness and fear was extreme but we knew they would not let us die.

Annalee's eyes were bulging in panic and she was burning through whatever oxygen she had managed to take in before she was shoved off the boat. She was about ten yards away from me and I saw her go limp. It felt like an eternity as I swam quickly toward her.

I reached her as she began to descend into the

thirty-foot deep water and hauled her desperately to the surface.

As I burst up into the air, I was relieved to see the setting sun on the horizon. I inhaled deeply not realizing until that moment that I had not taken a breath since I dove down looking for her.

She was lifeless in my arms and I spun around looking for the Danger boat. I could now see it was about fifty yards away from me and under power. The captain of the boat was an old salt who had tossed a bunch of life rings over the side when I dove in to get Annalee. I grabbed one and put it over her head as the charter boat headed toward us.

I started to administer mouth to mouth just to get oxygen into her if possible until the boat could get her on board. In less that a minute, arms reached down from the starboard gunwale to drag us both onto Danger's deck.

It turned out one of the guests was an EMT from San Diego on vacation and he began to do CPR as the Captain radioed for emergency services. Suddenly Annalee puked up water, coughed and began to breathe on her own. She would live which was more than I could say for the sick fucker who threw her overboard tied up and gagged. *I made a promise to myself a similar fate was in his future.*

By the time the EMT boat arrived Annalee was sitting up and breathing almost normally. They checked her out and decided to take her to Lower Keys Medical for observation. I hitched a ride with them after thanking the Danger crew and guests particularly the EMT for saving her life. I promised free drinks for all at the *Mockingbird* on me during the rest of their stay in Key West. *Abacus would love that one.*

Once back on land, I was able to call Matt on a landline with an update and asked that he send a member of our security team to the hospital to keep an eye on Annalee. My phone was drowned during my little diving adventure so I would need a new one. In the meantime, I asked Matt to send Dale with one of his team down to pick me up at Lower Keys Medical. He would drop off a guard for Annalee and I would stay with her until they arrived.

The hospital insisted she stay overnight for observation and they gave her a sedative. She slept and I sat in the lobby waiting for Dale and the guard while I watched the Weather Channel.

In the meantime, Hurricane Margaret was heading west into the Caribbean Sea after dealing a glancing blow to the Cayman Islands. It had been upgraded to a Cat 4 with winds of one hundred and fifteen miles per hour being recorded with no sign of a let-up.

~ ~ ~

Dale arrived and I took him up to Annalee's room so his guy David could make sure no other attempt would be made on her life. We then headed back to the house, first stopping briefly at Hog Fish for takeout sandwiches and a pit stop to pick up a new phone. My first call was to Digger.

"Hey Finn, wha's up?" he answered.

"I have a question for you. What is GG saying about the Hurricane coming across Cuba?"

"I don't know but here, ask her yourself. We just finished dinner at the new Seven Fish. You have to take Stacy to check out the Seafood Marinara Pasta. Hang on, here she is."

"Well Hello, Finn." said a sultry voice, "If you haven't been here yet, you need to try it. Great food," she raved. "As far as Margaret is concerned, with any luck, she will turn north, the tourists will all leave and the rest of us can stick around for the Hurricane parties."

"What's your gut tell you?" I continued.

"The next twelve hours will tell. If Margaret turns north now, she will hit Cuba south of Havana. It's bad for them but better for us as she will break up in the mountains and probably hit us as a tropical storm, possibly a Cat 1. If she gets into the Gulf, heats up and intensifies, then bounces off Yucatan, she could funnel up north of Cuba and we could be fucked."

I pressed her further. "What's your best guess?"

She paused then in a low voice said, "I ordered the crew to cancel our charters for the next few days, head out to the mangroves and tie her up. I've got almost a million bucks worth of boat there and I'd rather miss a few days of fishing with a safe boat than have to wait around for six months to collect insurance to get another one.

Her seriousness turned to fun as she teased, "Digger and I are going to make it a hurricane party by staying on board for the duration. There's nothing like hurricane sex, my friend. You should call Stacy and we can make it as foursome," she chuckled.

"GG, I'm tempted but I'm in the middle of something and need to see it through." *I sounded way too serious.*

"Well you know we're here for you. You might like it."

"Tempting, but I'm good thanks. Stay safe," and I hung up.

Ricardo was due in late tomorrow with his boat and crew so I decided to begin preparations for my little plan. The races were just ten days from now and we needed to be ready.

CHAPTER SIXTEEN

Matt, Hank and I spent the next two hours huddled together planning our next moves. I was also beginning to worry about Stacy. I had not heard from her since she left after seeing Annalee kissing me.

As we were wrapping up the plan for the next three days, Stacy came in and with barely an acknowledgment, immediately went to our room and locked the door. I followed her upstairs and knocked gently.

"Babe, can we talk?" I asked through the door. No response.

"Stacy, nothing happened between us. She was just saying goodbye," I maintained to no avail.

"Stacy, come on, you're being juvenile about this."

"Fuck you!" she shouted through the door. Maybe my choice was not the best turn of phrase.

"Come on, babe, at least we're now talking," throwing in some positive spin.

Nothing. Okay, last resort.

"Stacy, I'm sorry. I know you're upset and the last thing I ever wanted is for you to feel angry or disappointed in me."

I heard soft sniffles through the door.

"Babe, I screwed up. Please give me a chance to make it up to you. I promise," I added pulling out all the stops.

"Go away and we will talk tomorrow," was all I got. Well, at least it was a start. It looked like tonight would be a sofa night.

Actually, I found an empty room off the kitchen that I assumed was for a cook or housekeeper but it looked as if in had not been occupied for a while so I claimed it.

~ ~ ~

I lay down and the next thing I knew I was waking up to the smell of breakfast cooking. I guess Matt and Dale had decided to take me out of the rotation for guard duty.

After a quick shower in the bathroom off the kitchen, I threw on a robe I found in the closet. I helped myself to a tray with coffee and piled two plates with eggs and sausage that Consuelo had whipped up. I carried the tray up to Stacy and knocked gently then finding the door surprisingly unlocked.

I quietly opened it and found a Glock pointed at my head, Stacy standing naked on the other end. "Room Service?" I offered, meekly raising an eyebrow. She lowered the gun, took the tray and sauntered seductively over to the bed. *I could watch reruns of that view all day.* She set the tray on an ottoman, took a sausage and slowly put one end in her mouth. She still had not said a word.

I could feel myself begin to stiffen against the folds of my robe. She then took a rather aggressive bite off the end of the sausage. The symbolism was not lost on me. She smiled and climbed into bed.

After half an hour we were both left panting and covered in a fine sheen of sweat, not to mention famished. Through the door, we heard a round of applause. Assholes I thought, but she laughed.

"Get out of here so I can finish my now cold breakfast and take a shower." They were the first words she had spoken since I came into the room. I gathered up my robe and dutifully headed down the stairs, my knees just a little shaky. Makeup sex is a beautiful thing.

The TV was on in the kitchen and the table was crowded with about six of Dale's guys plus Matt and Hank.

"Margaret has slowed down to about eight miles per hour and is moving northwest." Matt began, "If she keeps on that course she could just graze the coast of Cuba then turn into the Straits. We could get the outer bands in the next eighteen hours then get slammed in less than twenty-four."

Matt continued, "Also Ricardo called and he is due here in about ten hours. His guys called while you were . . ." he paused, " . . . delivering breakfast."

"Fuck off," I said with a sizable smile.

"He's outside of Orlando and traffic is light in this direction but jammed heading north. Let's hope he makes it before they close the road south."

"They have ordered all tourists out in a mandatory evacuation," Hank added. "Margaret is still a Cat 3 but now with sustained winds of a hundred and ten miles an hour."

This was not my first rodeo.

"Okay, we have a lot to do in the next six hours. Dale, we are going to need your guys to pick up some things before supplies run low in town." I took out my new phone and pulled up the list I kept of hurricane supplies needed for emergencies.

"Hank, I just emailed you my list of preparations and the supplies we'll need. Can you compare it with what you already have then take two or three guys out to get the rest?"

I turned to Matt. "This house has hurricane windows that should be fine but I need to get down to

Catherine Street and put up the hurricane shutters around my place. Can you do a sweep around here and the garage to check for any loose furniture, trash bins and garden equipment that can get blown around if we get a serious blow? Also, check the palms for coconuts and take them down if you can. A coconut in a hundred and twenty-five mile an hour wind can hit like a cannonball."

~ ~ ~

We all spent the next three hours racing around town getting supplies, putting up shutters and tying down anything that could become a missile. The city was slowly becoming a ghost town of boarded-up buildings and hurricane parties in full swing behind the plywood. *Blowjobs by Margaret $5* and *Bite me Margaret* were spray painted on the plywood covering the windows at 801 Bourbon Bar.

With the tourists all but gone, many restaurants and bars hosted seventy-five percent off food and half-price booze in the event that power was off for an extended period of time. Rather than have food spoil, they might as well get something for it. We call it the 'Locals Appreciation Party'.

Intrepid locals were out blowing conch shells in an effort to ward off Margaret in keeping with the old superstition that the sound will ward off hurricanes.

In Old Town, Conchs were lighting candles at the Lourdes Grotto on the grounds of Saint Mary's Basilica. Catholic nuns built the shrine after the 1919 Hurricane claimed six hundred lives in Key West. The dedication reads, *As long as the Grotto stands, Key West will never experience the full brunt of a Hurricane.* I stopped there on my way back to Shark Key to light a candle. *Couldn't hurt.*

We all gathered back at the house around noon for updates and food. All the prep was done at the house on Catherine with patio furniture stored and aluminum shutters put up. Prep was going well at Shark Key as well. Hank had come rolling in with a truckload of supplies from extra propane and water to cases of wine, batteries, rice, beans plus an extra generator for the garage.

Dale had gone over to Southernmost Guns on Stock Island for ammunition and came back with three cases of nine mm, a case of .40 for my USP 40 and a case of M855A1 ammo for the M4 and two .300 boxes for the sniper rifle.

"Jesus, Dale are you expecting a war?" I inquired.

All he said was, "Better too much than too little."

"Did you get the tarps I asked for?"

"Yes I cleaned out Home Depot, but why you need so many I don't understand."

"I'll explain later but for now put them in the garage with the extra generator and the ammo, thanks."

Consuelo was in the midst of baking some kind of Brioche smoked ham, Havarti and Dijon sandwiches with a brown sugar glaze. *Damn that woman could cook.*

"Consuelo, I could kiss you," said one of Dale's men as he reached for a second sandwich. It seemed he hadn't been briefed on her recent gender shift. Or maybe he had?

She smiled seductively and said, "Handsome, only if you think you could handle it," and he blushed.

"Hey turn up the TV," shouted someone as Jim Cantore came on the Weather Channel.

"Hurricane Margaret is continuing her erratic path south of the Cayman Islands but heading northwest toward the Yucatan Peninsula. She continues to gain strength and now has sustained winds of one hundred and thirty miles an hour. The concern is that she will turn north or even northeast and score a hit on Cuba near Havana."

"We're only ninety miles from Havana," one of our guards said. "Does that mean it will hit us?"

I decided to add a bit of local color.

"Actually hurricane forecasting hasn't really advanced that much in the last twenty-five years. Even with all the satellites, hurricane spotter planes and computer modeling, the forecasters can expect a storm to veer as much as a hundred and ten miles off its projected course in a twenty-four hour period."

Continuing the lesson, I added, "If it turns north we could expect to get the outer bands in the next twelve hours." What I didn't say was that even if it weakened over Cuba, we could still be hit by at Cat 2 hurricane.

A Category 2 hurricane can have sustained winds of up to a hundred and ten miles an hour and do significant damage to roofs and shallow rooted trees. Flooding in low-lying areas can also cause power outages and debris fields that block roads. Okay, enough of the scary stuff."

~ ~ ~

We had not heard from *Blunt Force* and I wondered how long it would take them to figure out that the formula in the notebook was missing a vital ingredient. The enzyme for this process is sort of like the yeast in a loaf of bread. Without it, you get unleavened bread or in this case, useless fuel.

Meanwhile, Hank was testing the biofuel for octane levels and seemed happy with the results.

"The tests are really promising," he announced enthusiastically. "Using E90 fuel made with this process, we will increase the horsepower while reducing the cost of the fuel. It improves engine efficiency and contrary to popular myth has minimal corrosive effects. We have also hit the 112 octane level we need, I can't wait to test it in the boat. I think we can get a ten percent boost in speed and acceleration at a lower burn rate. It should be a game changer," he declared excitedly.

"Hank," I interrupted. "My question for you is how long do you think it will take Blunt Force to figure out they are missing an ingredient for the process?"

He thought for a moment then said, "If they send it to an outside lab they will probably take up to forty-eight hours to test the usual enzymes and realize they are missing something. My uncle was not only a brilliant chemist but he understood biochemistry. If they are using chemists from Dupree Chemical they may not understand how enzymes interact with different substrates and rates of reaction to create biochemical reactions."

My eyes started to gloss over.

"He identified a specific enzyme found in the anaerobic gut fungi of goats and camels that enable the breakdown of complex substrates like hemp. I was able to get a stock of the fungi before I got the notebook so I could do the testing once I had his formula."

"So, you lost me at anaerobic but if I'm getting the basics unless they have an army of biochemists working on it, we are at least forty-eight hours ahead of them before they feel the need to come after us again. Right?"

As he shrugged his shoulders he said, "A safe assumption."

Stacy who had been sitting quietly listening to all this said, "Hank have you filed a patent for this process yet?"

"Hardly, I just figured it out this morning," he answered.

"Okay, before we do anything, we need to get an

application submitted immediately."

"Stacy I know you have his best interests at heart but we have a hurricane bearing down on us, a team of hired mercenaries trying to kill us and I have two potential murder charges hanging over my head. Can't the legal stuff wait?" I requested.

"Finn, you do the derring-do, heroic, and macho stuff. Let me make sure Hank can benefit from all your efforts."

"I love it when you talk derring-do," I quipped.

"Hank, go with Stacy and figure out what legal stuff you need to do and we'll work on the rest."

They headed off to Hank's makeshift lab in the garage.

"Matt, have we heard from Ricardo?"

"Yes, He's making good time and is now south of Miami. He should be here in about four hours."

"Okay, great. By the way, I'm concerned Edwin 'Whiner' King from Blunt Force may move faster than we expect. I want to give him something to think about."

"What do you have in mind?" he asked.

I told him and he laughed.

An hour later my phone rang and it was OJ fuming. "Finn, You really know how to piss people off," he began.

CHAPTER SEVENTEEN

"Really? To you of all people, this can't be news."

"No, but some guy named Edwin King was surprised."

I chuckled. "What did he say?"

"Well, first he denied having any idea what we were talking about, then he asked for his lawyer."

"We next searched the house and we found the envelope that you said had the thumb drive in it. We then found the thumb drive with the WWF logo on it. It had been wiped but the logo ties them to the theft you mentioned on the phone."

"He denied having any knowledge of the drive or the envelope. We can at least hold he and his crew for twelve hours and maybe with the storm max twenty-four until he is released by a judge."

"Now tell me, what is this all about?" OJ then asked.

"I gave him an abbreviated version of the notebook being on the *Kilimanjaro* and the kidnapping of Annalee to get the notebook."

"Finn, do you think Annalee will be able to identify her kidnappers? If she could, it's a much bigger case than just robbery."

I told him I doubted it as King was not stupid and probably had his crew keep their faces covered. He sounded a bit crestfallen so I thought he needed some encouragement.

"One thing you might want to check is the storage facility on Catherine Street for anything registered in the name of King or Blunt Force. I think you'll find at least a stash of weapons with possibly RPGs."

He seemed to reenergize a bit with that, thanked me and hung up his phone to head back out before the storm arrived.

With that, I gave Matt an update and again we checked on the storm. It was beginning to turn toward Havana. *Shit.*

Well at least I had been able to get Blunt Force off our backs for a few hours and we could finish up plans for my next little magic trick.

For the next three hours, Matt and I spent our time putting the finishing touches on Hank's boat. He had built a beautiful forty-eight-foot Victory-designed Catamaran with twin twelve hundred and fifty horsepower Mercury engines and a gleaming paint job. The stern one-third was a dark green to symbolize the carbon negative construction and fuel from its power plants. The middle third was a glossy white with space for sponsors' logos and the front third was a bright red to match the color of his Smokin' Hot Hemp Car. *For some reason, the color scheme seemed very familiar.*

We covered the entire boat with the tarps we had brought in and strapped them down completely. We expected Ricardo to arrive at any time.

About ten minutes later, we heard the rumble of a heavy Cummins diesel coming down the street in Shark Key. I looked up to see Ricardo pulling up in his up-armored Porsche Cayenne Turbo followed by his big rig towing his racing Superboat. Behind the first rig was a second rig carrying parts, spares, and his full machine shop. *I'm sure the neighbors loved us.*

Ricardo hopped out of his Porsche, came over to me and threw his arms up. In each hand, he had one of the plain unlabeled bottles of his family's private Tequila stock.

"We are here mi amigo, how can we help?" he boomed.

"Ricardo, my friend you made it just in time," and I led him into the house. I took out glasses for tequila shots and he poured while I again turned up the TV. The news was not good.

The outer bands of Hurricane Margaret were just reaching Nueva Gerona, an island south of Cuba. That put it at about a hundred and ninety-five miles from Key West. Hurricane hunter aircraft put the storm at eighty miles in diameter so that put the eye of the hurricane about forty miles further away. Margaret was now a Cat 3 with sustained winds of a hundred and twenty-five miles per hour and Key West was in the target cone. The target cone or in reality, the *Cone of Uncertainty* is often displayed as a graphic showing the possible range of directions a hurricane travels over the next several days.

Assuming it stayed on course and continued to travel at about eight to ten miles per hour, winds could start to pick up some time tomorrow morning. We could be in for eight to ten hours of hurricane force winds during the day tomorrow. We needed to work fast.

I raised my glass and said, "My friend, it looks like we are in for a blow tomorrow so I propose a toast. May the prayers to the Lourdes Grotto in Key West be answered, that never again will Key West bear the full brunt of a hurricane."

We both drank to that and while he poured another shot, I laid out my plan just as Matt, Hank, and Stacy came in. After warm greetings all around and another toast, I walked everyone through what I wanted to do. I was going to need Ricardo to buy in big time.

"Ricardo, Hank has built a Victory-designed forty-eight-foot Unlimited Class Super Boat. What makes it unique is the body is made from hemp and titanium woven fiber that is stronger than carbon fiber and Kevlar glass that is used in traditional boats in this series. Also, the engines will run on a biofuel made from hemp."

I continued as I clearly had his full attention. "We plan on running it in the Super Boat World Championships Unlimited Class in ten days. Here is the problem. We believe Dupree Petroleum has hired the mercenary contracting firm Blunt Force run by an ex-Navy Seal Edwin King to prevent the development of the fuel and in fact to steal the formula.

Matt with help from his friend Dale from WWF have so far prevented the theft and we have been able to temporarily get the Blunt Force guys arrested."

Ricardo was sitting dumbfounded as we brought him up to speed. I continued, "So far they have killed two people including one of their own and one of Dale's men and we suspect they killed the cousin of a friend of mine." I glanced at Stacy who simply smiled thinly. *Too soon I suppose.*

I decided to leave out the kidnapping of Annalee and the potential murder charges against me for the moment.

"We are going to need to protect the boat for the next ten days and during the race. Here is what I have in mind."

As I walked through the plan, everyone in the room fell silent and Ricardo's eyes got bigger and bigger. In the end, as a beautiful sunset played out on the horizon, he simply said, "I'm in."

~ ~ ~

The next five hours were a whirlwind of activity, pun intended. Ricardo's crew fired up the big rig hauling the parts trailer and backed it into the garage and hooked up Hank's boat and trailer hauling it out into the drive. The matching rig then backed Ricardo's boat into the garage. The crew then scrambled to remove the engines from Ricardo's boat. Using the same color scheme as Hank had used on his boat's hull, they painted the damaged boat. Finally, we planned to cover the boat in the morning as soon as the paint dried with matching tarps. We now had what would appear, at least upon a cursory look, to be two matching Super Boat Unlimited Class forty-eight-foot Catamarans.

Dale's crew set up a perimeter team covering any view of the property from the ocean and the road using the trailers large sail-shaped awnings to hide our activity. While I hoped that all of the Brunt Force crew was still locked up, I could not be certain and I needed to create confusion regarding the boats.

Exhausted, we took a final look at the weather before crashing for the night. The outer bands were heading almost due north between the Sierra de Los Organos Mountains in the northwest of Cuba and the city of Havana. If Margaret, currently a Category 3 storm turned slightly to the northeast, Key West was in the bullseye.

Before heading to bed I took Crutch on a walk around the property, in part to check all our preparations but also I felt like he and I had not spent a lot of time together in the last few days. I opened a Bud Light for him after our walk and after filling his bowl I gave him a quick rub behind the ears and headed to bed.

As I climbed in beside a sleeping Stacy I heard him pad into the room and flop by the door. I took it as a sign we were good. I still need to get him laid I thought as I drifted off to sleep.

I awoke with a start to sun streaming in the window and the sky burned crimson.

There is an old sailor adage that goes, "Red sky at

night, sailor's delight; Red sky in the morning, sailors take warning."

My glance out the window showed that the latter was in play. The eastern sunrise was a burning red and orange. Not a good sign.

Crutch opened his eyes as I rose and slowly stretched. Stacy was still sleeping so Crutch and I headed first for my morning pee then I sent him out for his. I fired up the coffee pot and turned up the volume on the TV to hear Jim Cantore once again on the Weather Channel.

"Hurricane Margaret has been downgraded to a Category 1 hurricane after passing over Cuba and is now maintaining its course north toward the Dry Tortugas. It appears that Key West will be spared the worst of the storm but as they say, "It's never over till it's over.

Thanks a bunch Jim. I'm always tempted to blame him when he's wrong about a storm as if in some way he has control of it. I remember seeing a weather reporter during one storm, standing under a downspout just off-camera, trying to convince the audience that he was in the midst of a deluge. In the distance, you could see a surfer having a great time.

Things still seemed uncertain so I poured a coffee for me and a bowl of food for Crutch then went out on the porch for a moment's peace.

My time in the Keys had been anything but uneventful. Between the events of the last few years and this latest drama, I was beginning to consider the need to rethink my life. The thing is, it seems that you can never escape your past. We appear to drag it around with us like a string of heavy chains that weigh us down. I remembered a Charles Dickens quote from *A Christmas Carol* I read as a kid.

"I wear the chain I forged in life," replied the Ghost.

"I made it link by link, and yard by yard; I girded it on of my own free will, and of my own free will I wore it."

~ ~ ~

I had hoped for a new start when I married Courtney and moved to the Rock. Now she was dead and I was a disgraced cop whose best friend was a three-legged dog.

"Fuck!" I shouted at the world.

I hate it when I get all maudlin and feeling sorry for myself.

You have a very hot, super smart girlfriend, great friends like Ricardo, Abacus, Matt, and Hank plus you live in an island paradise. So what's the issue?

Something was bugging me but I couldn't put my finger on it. Crutch joined me and we stared out over the ocean waiting for Margaret to make up her mind.

The sun rose higher in the sky and the house began to stir with sounds of Consuelo in the kitchen and various bodies coming downstairs, pouring coffee and stumbling outside a little stiff from yesterday's physical efforts.

Hank came over to the table where I was sitting. "What do you think?"

"About what?" I replied.

"The plan and the storm. Is there something else I should be thinking about? he asked.

"I think the first two are enough for now."

"Okay, so?" he continued.

"The storm is the unknown. If it shifts to the east and picks up speed, all bets are off. A direct hit from a Category 3 could flood as much as six feet or more of water on top of the island. In addition to the flooding, we could have tin roofs careening around like giant guillotines, trees toppled blocking roads and two by fours flying like blunt spears punching through walls and even people."

"Jesus," was all he said.

"Actually you're right, *Jesus*. If our prayers are answered, it stays going north or even a bit west. The mountains in Cuba should create some weakening and between the two we might *only* get a Cat 1 with the outer east side bands of the storm. Wind speeds of eighty-five to ninety miles an hour are still damaging and dangerous but not as lethal."

"Okay, and the plan?"

"Well, this morning Ricardo's crew is going to move your boat down to the Truman Waterfront where the boats for the races have begun to stage. The race organizers have set up a special area in the old concrete Navy maintenance facility for the crews to secure their boats and equipment. It should withstand winds of up to one hundred miles an hour but above that, all bets are off."

"And what about Ricardo's boat?" he asked.

"We are going to leave it in the garage for now as bait for the *Blunt Force* guys."

I began to feel a freshening of the breeze and hurried into the kitchen. Jim Cantore was again on the Weather Channel with an update.

"Hurricane Margaret currently downgraded to a Category 1 continues on its path north. It is headed about thirty miles east of Dry Tortuga, which is seventy miles off the tip of Key West. The outer bands are about two hours away from the Tortugas and we should expect the eye to pass between the Tortugas and Key West. At this point, Key West should be spared a direct hit but remember the worst wind damage is generally on the Northeast quadrant of the storm."

"Okay guys, it's time to move the rigs down to the waterfront. We have about two hours before we get hit."

Ricardo scrambled his crew and began firing up

both the parts rig and the boat rig, checking the tarps and the fifth wheel.

Hank and I jumped into the Mustang to drive ahead of the rigs and keep an eye on things plus to clear the rigs into the staging area.

The wind was beginning to blow at about thirty miles an hour and would only get worse. We sped down U.S. 1 and over Cow Key Bridge.

We paused to again check the weather on the radio as the rigs radioed that they were just leaving Shark Key. I decided to take A1A down South Roosevelt past the airport to get a clean sighting the south side of the island and any flooding.

Over the radio, Ricardo called out, "Finn, somebody just blew up my fucking boat."

CHAPTER EIGHTEEN

"Say again!" I shouted over the radio.

"Somebody just blew up the boat!" he shrieked back at me.

"What do you mean? Where? How?"

"At the house, somebody fired an RPG at the garage from a go-fast boat off shore. It must have hit the fuel but the whole place went up."

"What about the house? Are Stacy and Matt okay?"

"Yes, they're fine. Stacy's directing Dale's crew to fight the fire and keep it contained to the garage. The boat and all the equipment are destroyed."

"How did they know to go after the boat in the garage?"

"I guess they tracked the plates on the trailers. They saw that the trailer leaving the house was mine, waited until we were clear then went after Hank's boat," suggested Ricardo.

"Shit, that was way faster than I expected them to work. Well, let's get the boat down to Truman Waterfront and into the staging area. This storm is going to be on us in no time."

I accelerated down South Roosevelt and was over to the Truman Waterfront in less than ten minutes. We checked in and waited for the rigs to show up.

Finally, forty-five minutes after leaving the house, the rigs pulled into the sheltered area inside the old

Navy blockhouse on the pier and out of the wind that was building steadily.

With the boat safely in place and with Ricardo's crew there to work on it, Hank and I sped back to the house.

As we pulled into Shark Key, we could see the fire trucks from Stock Island putting out some spot fires around the property but the main fire had burned the garage to the ground and scorched the house. With Margaret only a couple of hours away I expect any investigation will only come in the next day or so after the cleanup of the storm debris.

I saw Stacy sitting on the steps of the deck, her face streaked with black from the fire and her clothes covered in soot.

"Babe, are you okay?" I asked, concern clear in my tone.

"Truthfully, no," she began. "Finn, hanging around you is how I would imagine it's like living in a war zone. We have been together for what, a year now? In that time I've been kidnapped, almost blown up, shot at, and now just missed by an RPG. I used to never even know what an RPG was, for heaven's sake."

"Yeah but you have to admit it's never boring," I offered gently.

"Promise me when this is all over we can have a little boring. You know, a vacation villa in Aleppo or maybe a spa in Bagdad." She smiled and said, "I heard about a nice ski resort in Afghanistan."

"Well, as a matter of fact, I was considering all of those but settled on surfing in Somalia. Will that work for you?"

"Sounds like a hell of a vacation."

I decided to change gears. "Are you sure everyone is okay?"

Matt came around the corner and jumped in.

"Yeah, we were lucky. Consuelo spotted the go-fast boat coming in about five hundred yards off shore. She ran to the phone and called the guys working in there and they got out. She later said it appeared they fired from about two hundred yards out which makes it an easy shot. They must have hit the fuel storage tank next to the garage."

"I've put men all around what's left of the building so no one can inspect the wreckage. We don't need Blunt Force snooping around and figuring we had moved the boat."

"Don't worry, this storm is going to make that impossible for the next six to eight hours." I looked out over the ocean and the horizon had taken on a weird shade of dark gray-green and the wind was now beginning to howl.

I yelled, "We need to get inside. Now!"

Jim Cantore was back on the news, "Hurricane Margaret is just now reaching Key West." Shit, I thought. "She is moving slightly in a north-easterly direction picking up speed but Key West should be spared the worst of it. They can expect torrential rain and sustained winds of ninety miles per hour but the eye will miss the island by about thirty miles traveling between Key West and the Dry Tortugas."

~ ~ ~

The next six hours were a train wreck. Torrential rains pummeled the house and wreckage from the garage fire blew all around us. A loose propane tank flew into one of the hurricane windows shattering the tempered glass but not penetrating the window. Luckily the tank was empty and did not explode although any fire would have been both fed by the wind then doused by the rain.

The noise of a hurricane is like the sound of a freight train passing you as you stand beside the tracks.

The roar is deafening and the ground shakes. We could see pieces of tin roofs being ripped off neighbors' houses and siding being torn off the walls. I felt like Dorothy watching the bicycle-riding neighbor lady flying through the sky during the tornado scene in The Wizard of Oz. I could almost hear the music, da da da da da da. . . .

I am not sure what GG was talking about when she enthused about *hurricane sex* but all I could see was a vision of the roof being ripped off and being sucked out into the storm and hurtling down the street naked.

The winds blew and the rain came down in sheets pushed horizontally by the wind. The ocean seemed to rise up, then crash against the riprap surrounding the house at the shoreline. Each time the waves rose a little closer to swamping the lawn and tearing the dock from its pilings. A boat bimini, still attached to its frame, flew by then crashed into the house. Palm fronds filled the air as they sped by the windows at the side of the house.

The power failed and we waited, counting the seconds until the generator kicked in. The lights flickered then came on and the microwave beeped. The lights blinked on radios and appliances, cell phones had no signal and still, the winds rose to a crescendo that seemed to increase almost to a scream.

Toward the late afternoon, as we huddled in our respective corners of the house, someone wandered by to check on the others. Occasionally someone would venture from his or her individual safe spots to grab water, a beer or a quick sandwich.

It was during what I thought to be a lull that I realized that the wind had in fact diminished to merely deafening from primal scream. The rain was pelting rather than driving and a ray of sunlight seemed to peak between the black mountains of swirling clouds.

We began to congregate in the living room to compare stories from our various hiding spots around the house. A lawn chair was seen bouncing by a window into the darkness. The roof of a neighbor's dining pavilion torn from its foundations was seen disappearing into the sky. In one case a neighbor's cat, its claws embedded in a palm tree, was clinging for dear life, it's mouth open in an extended howl.

~ ~ ~

Since there was no cell service, I decided to try from our landline to reach Ricardo who was with his crew down at the Truman Waterfront with the big rigs and the boat.

I then called the *Mockingbird* to check on Abacus and a drunken voice answered, "Hag on, I'll fine him fur ya," then he hung up on me. I guess all was well after a fashion at the bar.

At this point, Crutch was bouncing on three legs to get out so I decided to take him to survey the damage. We forced our way out the door pushing back a pile of debris including; tree branches, palm fronds, a life preserver and an old tire.

We picked our way through the detritus from toppled and rolled garbage cans, palm fronds, and branches from stripped or torn up trees. Crutch was busy sniffing and selecting new spots to pee and I examined the cars, and roads to see if things were passable.

With the height of the storm now a receding memory, the earlier issues of boats to protect, murders to solve, my reputation to restore and races to win, we needed to renew our focus.

Fortunately, the house was high enough that it did not get flooded when the water rose onto the lawn. Less fortunate however was the Mustang that not only was flooded to the door panels but also had the windshield smashed by what appeared to the flying propane tank that hit the window in the house. I saw the cat that had been clinging to a palm tree during the storm walking delicately along a damaged fence looking wet and disoriented.

Several downed palm trees blocked the road out of Shark Key but I could already hear chainsaws being fired up by neighbors. I expect it will be passable in less than an hour. I pulled the propane tank out of the windshield and banged out the rest of the glass then started it up. I figured getting a car on the island in the next few days was going to be impossible and this was better than nothing.

Power was still out as was cell service. I went back into the house and using our landline called OJ at the station. He was out on calls so I just reported the attack on the garage and asked him to call me.

The sun was beginning to set and the sky in the west was a brilliant flaming orange, the air now crystal clear. Suddenly the TV station that had been nothing but snow and static came back on with Jim Cantore reporting on the now northerly threat to Tampa and the Redneck Riviera around Gulf Shores and Pensacola. Key West had avoided a direct hit and was an afterthought. We had come through the Category 1 Hurricane Margaret with no fatalities, some property damage and a power outage expected to last up to forty-eight hours.

I decided to call the hospital to check on Annalee. She answered on the third ring and her first concern after hearing it was me was to ask, "Finn, have you heard from my parents? They are going to be worried I am hurt. Can you call them?"

"Of course I can call them," I offered. "But can't you call them yourself?"

"No the hospital does not permit outbound

international calls, especially to Cuba. Plus I have a bit of a visa problem."

"A visa problem? Your credit card doesn't work? Just give them mine and you should be fine."

She laughed. "Not that kind of visa silly, my travel visa. I was given a three-day humanitarian visa to pick up Nieve and take her back to Cuba. I have overstayed it and the hospital reported me to the CBP."

"Jesus, in the middle of a hurricane they have nothing better to do than to come after you?" I cussed. "Let me see what I can do."

"In the meantime, I'll call your parents and let them know you're fine. I won't mention the kidnapping part."

We said goodbye and I went searching for Stacy.

I found her in the kitchen with Consuelo. Consuelo was showing Stacy how to disassemble, clean and maintain a Glock 19 then how to reassemble, load and store it safely. *It does a man's heart good to see his girl in the kitchen like that.*

I watched them for a bit then said, "Stacy when you finish can we chat? I need your help on something."

She nodded and said, "Give me five minutes to solo on this then I'll join you."

I headed to the living room as she began. She looked like a pro.

I sat on the sofa with Crutch trying to put the story of these events together. Amidst all the chaos of the storm, I had not had a chance to review everything that had happened in the last few days. Something was bugging me but I couldn't put my finger on it.

I remembered my experience in Iraq and Afghanistan. When something didn't feel right it was time to move. In combat, movement is life. You stand still you die. Stacy came into the room.

"That was fast," I said. "You're a quick study."

"I had a great teacher," she gushed. "Consuelo took it apart and put it back together blindfolded to show me how easy it was. I think I'll need some more practice before doing that though."

"Well, the next step is to get you on the range."

"We are already setting up a time to go." She smiled at me.

"Well before you go I have a favor to ask," I said with not a little trepidation. "I need your lawyer skills first."

"Okay what's up?" she asked. "You seem a little nervous."

I paused. "I have a friend with a little immigration problem."

Her eyes narrowed. "Go on."

"Stacy," I decided to jump in with both feet. "Annalee has been detained by the CBP for overstaying her visa. She was headed to the airport yesterday when a Blunt Force team guy abducted her. We had to get her back and she was hurt in the process. She couldn't leave because she was in the hospital."

I waited. And wondered, how did they know she was leaving? Was that what was bugging me?

"Okay," was all Stacy said.

"Look I know this is awkward for you and maybe a little uncomfortable but there is nothing between us."

"I believe you," she said quietly.

I breathed a sigh of relief, while still suspecting this was not over. "You are awesome."

Stacy went into her lawyer mode asking a bunch of questions then agreed to make some calls and see what she could do.

I leaned over to kiss her but she turned away.

Shit was all I could think of. "You're the best," was luckily what came out.

I then went in search of Matt and found him

166

examining the wreckage of the garage. Bits of charred carbon fiber boat and clumps of wiring melted together were all that remained of Ricardo's boat.

I had asked Ricardo to leave it in the garage while we took Hank's boat down to the staging area for the races and he had okayed it being used as a target but it still must have hurt. These things are not cheap.

"Matt, I want to talk about how we respond to this whole situation," I began.

"We're on the same page bro," he agreed. "I don't quite get why Blunt Force seems willing to kill to stop this boat from competing."

I nodded. "Go ahead, you first," was all I could say.

"Look, these guys are mercenaries used to fighting in war zones from Afghanistan to Zimbabwe. Why come to the U.S. and start killing people for some oil company? There is more than enough work all over the world without the chance of getting arrested in the States. It just doesn't make sense."

"I agree. Something about all this just doesn't add up plus I'm tired of being on defense all the time."

"What are you thinking?" he asked.

I walked him through my idea and he smiled. "Let's get Dale in on this to cover our six and provide critical mass."

CHAPTER NINETEEN

Consuelo who I last saw up to her elbows in gun oil and swabs cleaning an H&K USP 40, called out that dinner was ready.

How she had cleaned up the counter/workbench in the kitchen and laid out a feast, I have no idea. There were bowls of roasted brussels sprouts with bacon and pine nuts, roasted red skin garlic potatoes, and asparagus spears rolled in oil garlic and parmesan covering the counter like a Bacchanal feast. There was a platter of thick slices of Prime Rib and another of garlic shrimp plus bottles of red and white wines and homemade dinner rolls on the table.

It was then that I noticed it was almost nine o'clock and we'd not really eaten since the storm began almost ten hours ago. I was starving.

I grabbed a plate and piled heaps of veggies, beef, and shrimp then grabbed a glass to fill from a beautiful bottle of *Screaming Eagle* Cabernet. I sat down at the table. How had Consuelo done it? I didn't care I just wolfed it down as the others followed my lead and joined me.

For a while, the table was silent save the sound of utensils clattering on china, groans and the occasional shout of appreciation to Consuelo.

I again tried to reach Ricardo to see how he was and to let him know about our plans. There was still no cell service.

After dinner, Matt and I shared our plan with the group.

Key West is a small island. With communications by cell phone down, we figured unless Blunt Force was using sat phones they were as blind as we were but we couldn't rely on that assumption. If we decided to take Mohammad to the mountain so to speak, we needed to assume they would know we were coming.

Our only elements of surprise would be when, from what direction and in what strength.

I proposed we use the *Bright, Shiny Object Strategy*. This approach is to dangle a bright shiny object in front of an adversary while attacking them in a totally different place while they're distracted.

Assuming they were watching the house, we would load in the two Suburbans that Dale had brought down with him. Any watcher would see us going but not be sure what our target was going to be.

The roads should be passable enough to get through provided no bridge was out, or the flooding too deep along the coast after the storm.

We told everyone that we were going to go down to what we thought was the Blunt Force base in the storage facility on Catherine. In reality, Crutch, Stacy and I would take one of the Suburbans and go to the Catherine Street storage place. Matt would take the other one with six of Dale's crew and go the to Navy facility to check on Hank's boat.

Dale and Hank would stay behind at the house with Consuelo.

Our teams gunned up after three hours of sleep then headed out. We did not see anyone as we left the Shark Key gates but had to assume that we were being followed.

Driving down U.S. 1 was actually not too bad but with a lot of debris and flooding in some spots. When we got over Cow Key Bridge, Matt took a right onto North Roosevelt and I took a left driving over to Flagler.

It would have been difficult to follow both vehicles unless Blunt Force had two cars themselves. Neither of us saw any lights behind us.

I had decided the best approach was the direct approach so I drove to White Street then down Catherine pulling into the Self Storage driveway. I got out of the truck and began to bang on the door like a drunk who had lost his car keys and was trying to get into his house. There was no response. What a surprise. The tracker we had planted in the thumb drive was still beeping but nobody was home.

My assumption had been that after the cops detained the Blunt Force crew, as soon as they were released they would move their base of operations. Stacy and I were the shiny objects but being at Catherine Street was simple misdirection and probably the safest place for Stacy.

The bulk of the crew was at the boat primarily to protect it in the event that 'Whiner' and his crew went after it. Finally, on the off chance that they went after the house, Dale and Consuelo were there with Hank to keep him covered.

As I pounded on the door of the self-storage building I heard Crutch bark then I suddenly felt the cold steel barrel of a gun against the back of my neck.

"Don't move or turn around," growled a voice.

I felt the prick of a needle in my neck and I began to turn only to collapse. I caught sight of Stacy lying on the ground by the car as I fell.

The next thing I knew something was licking my face.

I tried to swat it away. "G'way," I mumbled.

Slowly I opened one eye. I had a splitting headache.

Drugs or fall I wondered?

Where was I, where was Stacy and what time was it? "St...y?" I called out still not able to form words. It was pitch dark and very hot.

Crutch came up and licked me again.

"Go away and let me sleep," I moaned.

I must have passed out again and when I came around, there was a sliver of light under one wall. It must be morning.

My head was a bit better and I could see I was not alone in the room. Crutch stirred beside me and I could see Stacy lying on the floor. The light under the wall turned out to be a roll-up door of corrugated metal. This was starting to look like a locker in the self - storage facility.

"Well this is another fine mess you've gotten us into Stanley," came the disembodied voice of Stacy.

I laughed and winced. "You're welcome, Ollie. Are you okay?"

"If you call a splitting headache and hurt pride okay, then yes, I'm okay. And you?"

"Same."

"Where do you think we are?" Stacy asked.

"If I had to guess, we're in the storage locker they were using as a base of operations. I imagine they took longer to clean out than I expected."

Then after a pause, "Or they got tipped off that we were headed here."

"Tipped off? By who?" she asked.

"Your guess is a good a mine."

"So how do we get out of here? We've lost at least four or five hours," she speculated.

I struggled to my knees, let a wave of nausea pass then slowly stood up while leaning against the wall. From what I could see in the dim light the locker was about eight feet deep by eight feet wide with cinder block walls and a roll up door. I went over to the door and pounded on it making a booming sound that exploded in my head.

"Jesus," Stacy said shortly. "What the hell did they give us?"

"I have no idea but at least we aren't dead."

Stacy struggled to her feet and came over to the door. She leaned over and pushed up. The door slid open.

"I think I found our escape plan," she smirked.

We walked out through the crash bar on the door with an exit sign and saw our truck in the parking lot. The keys were in it.

My gun was missing but the cell phone was still in its charger on the dash. I had fifteen missed calls but at least I now had a signal.

I called Matt.

"Dude, where have you been?" was his opening line.

"Stacy and I decided to have early morning room service at the Saint Hotel on Eaton then a quick roll in the hay was in order. What'd I miss?"

"Very funny. Where are you now?"

I filled him in then asked, "My question still stands, what'd I miss?"

"I'm at the house. You'd better get up here. Dale's been shot and may not make it. Hank and Consuelo are missing. The house has been trashed."

CHAPTER TWENTY

"Jesus. I'll be there in fifteen minutes.

I fired up the truck and backed out of the parking lot. Tearing up Catherine toward White we listened on speaker as Matt described his night.

"We got down to the Waterfront where we parked the boat in the Navy maintenance building and all was quiet. Ricardo had his team covering the perimeter and things seemed under control. Without cell service, I waited about an hour when suddenly service was restored. I checked messages and one was a frantic call from Hank."

He said, "The house was under attack by people who looked like the ones from the night Stacy was hit by glass. Dale had been hit and Consuelo was trying to keep them at bay. Oh shit, was the last thing Hank said then he was cut off.

"I called the cops and took off with two of Dale's guys to see if I wasn't too late. We got there about five and it was a mad house. Cops were all over the place and the ambulance was loading Dale. He had been shot in the head and was unconscious. The house was cleared but Hank and Consuelo were gone. I tried to reach you but you were AWOL."

I was beginning to get pissed. This guy Edwin 'Whiner' King was proving to be better than we'd anticipated. We had tried to take the initiative and he had just totally kicked our ass.

My cell rang. "Who the fuck is this?" I shouted at the unknown caller.

"No need for names Finn, did you get my message?"

"I don't talk to people with no name." I hung up then listened to my messages ignoring the next two calls.

The tenth message was, "Mr. Pilar, or can I call you Finn? My employer wanted you to know that your friends will be staying with us as our guests until the races are finished. You will continue with your racing preparation but you will lose if you hope to see your friends again. If you question our sincerity check your text messages and the picture should provide you with a sense of our hospitality."

I swiped over to messages and saw a picture of Hank having been beaten. Blood was covering his face, one eye was swollen shut and his head drooped as he sat tied to a Chair drooling spit and blood.

The phone rang again. The screen read *Unknown Caller.*

I answered, "Listen asshole. . ."

He hung up.

It's irritating to be on the other end of that, I have to admit.

I waited.

It rang again. "What?"

"I am assuming you got my messages and my text" he began.

I gritted my teeth. "Yes," I growled.

"They say a picture is worth a thousand words." He paused. "I wonder what a body part is worth?" He hung up.

Who is this guy I wondered? *The voice sounded vaguely familiar.*

This was becoming a huge cluster fuck. The only

apparent good news is that it appeared Hank's boat would be safe. It seemed that a) they knew the boat was still safe - probably Hank had been forced to tell them, and b) they would rather have the boat lose the race than destroy it.

I called Ricardo and asked him to come up to Shark Key for a race team meeting. "Can you also bring Hector from Dale's team up as well. Thanks."

With Consuelo absent, it fell on me to make breakfast while we waited for Ricardo, Hector, the team's driver, and their throttle man to get to Shark Key. I liked to think while I was cooking.

I threw two-dozen eggs in a large skillet after browning some leftover chopped roast potatoes, some onion and a pound of Jimmy Dean pork sausage. I smothered it in some aged white cheddar cheese and put it in the oven. While it was cooking, I heated some of the leftover dinner rolls and it was all ready by the time they arrived.

With hot coffee and a belly full of *Breakfast Casserole a la Pilar*, we went into the living room to discuss the races and the messages from the *Asshole*.

After some understandable ranting and raving, we got down to business.

"My thinking goes like this," I started.

"We need to divide into four teams. Red team, focus on the boat including preparation and testing. Green team, focus on fuel and we will need to produce it in record time using a boatload of hemp waste. Blue team, provide security for the boat and the house. Finally, we need the Black team to find and extract Hank so we can actually win this race."

"Questions? Comments?"

Matt jumped in with the first question. "Who needs to lead the teams?" This was a good start, as the group seemed to accept the basics of what I just outlined.

"Good question," I replied. "What do you think?"

"If it were me deciding, I would say, Ricardo for the Red team, you on Green, Hector on Blue and I will take Black."

"Ricardo, Hector what do you think?' I asked.

They both nodded in agreement.

"Hector, any word on Dale?" I inquired.

"I called on the way here and he was going into surgery. The nurse said he came to in the ambulance and it looks like his head is harder than we thought. The bullet actually tore his cheek and took out some teeth but it didn't go into his brain. He fell when it happened and was knocked out." After a moment, he added, "His wife is going to be pissed with the new scar."

"That's great but it looks like he will be out of action."

"Don't count on it," was Hector's response.

"Okay." I changed gears. "I will need some help on this fuel thing. I have no idea where to find the ingredients and get them here but I think Digger can help with the chemistry."

"Ricardo, are you good?" I asked.

"Yes, no worries amigo," he replied. "Also, I may be able to help with the hemp. My plane can carry loads in from growers I know in Kentucky and if necessary Oregon and California. I'll call them while we head down to the Waterfront to get the boat lined up on the schedule."

"That is awesome my friend. Muchas, muchas gracias."

He headed out the door calling out, "It's going to be crazy after the hurricane and I need my guys to check out this boat and start putting it through its paces."

"Hector?" I asked, "Are you good with the boss out?"

"Piece of cake. In fact, I called already and we've got six more guys coming in this afternoon. With the boss out of action for the moment, I have full authority to take over."

"Perfect, let me know if you need anyone else on your team."

"Actually I do," he said. "I'd like to get Stacy on my team. She has great local knowledge of both the city and the surrounding islands."

I wanted to say, "No fucking way. She has been through enough already today and it's not even noon," but fortunately it was only a thought bubble.

My better angels said, "Stacy, are you good with that role?"

She smiled at me as if to say, "I saw your thought bubble," then she said, "Sounds like fun."

I turned to where Matt had been sitting and said, "Matt, are you all set?" but he was already gone.

"I guess so," I remarked as the others took off on their assignments.

"Stacy," I called out. "Before you go. . . ." I paused.

She said, "I talked to my firm in Tampa and they are sending a guy down to talk to Annalee as soon as the storm blows past. It doesn't look like it will hit Tampa. In the meantime, she has been released from the hospital and is coming back to the house."

The look on my face must have been enough because she said, "You're welcome," then came over and gave me a big smile followed by a long, passionate kiss.

"You behave yourself while she's here and I'll have a surprise for you later," and she turned to leave.

"Stay safe out there, babe. And you know how much I love surprises."

It was time for me to get to work. With Ricardo working on finding a source for the hemp waste product, I called Digger to ask for his help.

"Finn, my man, wha's up?" he answered. "How's it hangin'?"

"Sorry Digger, I'm still swinging on the straight side dude. How was your hurricane ride? Did GG make it a rough one?"

"A gentleman never tells, my man," he answered. "All good with you?"

"Actually I could use your help," I began.

I brought him up to speed and finally outlined my request. "Digger, I was never much for chemistry and I am tasked in Hank's absence with using his formula to produce the fuel for the races. I could use your help in putting together the lab and getting the right mix to make it happen. Can you help?"

"Finn, I'm happy to help but you should know I was a C student in chemistry. Even that was because I screwed the professor so he would give me the test ahead of time. You might say there was a certain chemistry between us, " he quipped.

"Digger that's more than I need to know. My question is, do you remember enough to help?"

"Sure" was all he said.

"Okay, thanks," I said gratefully.

"I'm going to email a copy of the file from a thumb drive Hank used to make the test batch. Take a look at it and tell me what we are going to need to make two hundred and fifty gallons of the fuel."

"Okay, I'm on it. GG and I are almost back from our little hurricane sausage party. We are sailing into the harbor now so I should be able to get back to you within an hour." He hung up.

I sent him the file that Hank was working from then began looking for hemp fiber sources on my own. The more I dug into the subject, the more I realized two things.

The first was that Hank was really on to something with the idea of using hemp fiber as a biofuel feedstock and secondly, we would never be able to make enough fuel using his formula in the time before the races. It required a multi-step fermentation process using specialized equipment that in our case had been destroyed in the fire in the garage.

Digger called as I was reading more about the production process. "Finn, I appreciate your confidence in my chemistry skills but this is not going to happen."

I must have sounded desperate when I said, "Nothing is impossible Digger. What are the issues?"

He paused to collect his thoughts then said, "Look, the first issue is a qualified biochemist with enough time could put together what's needed but this process requires specialty equipment like low ultrasound pulse technology for fermentation of specific enzymes. It's available from a company in South Africa but getting it here is next to impossible.

The second issue is volume. I did a couple of quick calculations based on the specs for the two engines in the boat and they burn roughly three hundred gallons an hour. These races usually take from start to finish plus warm up, sixty minutes. So let's say you need three hours for total racing plus you are going to have to do shakedowns and prep etcetera. You are going to need roughly two thousand gallons to cover yourselves."

This was not what I wanted to hear.

"The third issue is you also need legal access to hemp waste feedstock which is currently not legal in Florida."

When he said Florida, something clicked. "Okay Digger, you've given me an idea. I'll get back to you."

At that moment, Annalee came running into the house and when she saw me, came over and planted a big kiss on me. I could feel a little celebration chubby forming but my better angels kicked into gear and I remembered the promised surprise from Stacy.

"Whoa, there tiger," I said perhaps with a tinge of regret in my voice. "I'm glad I could help but it was really Stacy who made it happen."

"Finn, if it weren't for you I might have been stuck in that awful place for weeks," she said with a twinkle in her eye. "I owe you."

I took a deep breath. "No, I owe you. I seemed to have gotten you into this mess and you are welcome to stay here until you can take Nieve home. I know your parents must be worried."

She smiled a little seductively but said, "You're right," then she sighed.

"I need to take a shower," she said with a leer. "Then I can make some lunch for everyone but after that let me know what I can do for you." She turned and left the room with a little shake of her ass.

She has a great ass. To keep me honest, I said to myself out loud, "Down boy, get back to work."

I settled down and went back through my research. After a few minutes, I found the reference I was looking for. There was a company in Canada that had developed a pilot program for making ethanol using hemp waste as feedstock. Maybe the solution was not to produce the fuel using Hank's exact process but simply to buy some hemp-based biofuel already being made.

After a couple of false starts, I again found the article on the pilot program and called the company. Eventually, I was connected to the Business Development Manager, aka the head sales guy, and told him what I wanted.

"Can you produce two thousand gallons of 112 Octane racing fuel in the next six days?"

"Sir we are a research company that produces about three hundred gallons a day for test vehicles in our program. What you are asking for is impossible."

"Look, I will pay you one hundred dollars a gallon for all you have and all you can produce. I can pick up the first load in twelve hours."

I could almost see him doing the math in his head. "Can I put you on hold?" he asked.

I waited impatiently while the company did the math and looked at their inventory, feedstock and production schedules.

After ten minutes of cooling my heels, the CEO of the company came on the line. "This is Grayson Roberts, CEO of SynGas. To whom am I speaking?"

He sounded so formal so I switched into my respectful mode, "Grayson, my man. This is Finn Pilar with . . . . " Shit, I needed to make up a company. "With Mockingbird Racing in Key West." *Not bad for spur of the moment I thought.*

"We are pilot testing a new hemp/titanium constructed offshore racing boat and our fuel supplier experienced a catastrophic fire in their plant, pun intended," I chuckled.

When I heard him laugh, I knew I had him. "We are trying to prove that hemp ethanol can be competitive with petroleum-based fuels and we need your help."

After another pause, he said, "Mr. Pilar, we have about one thousand gallons of the fuel you requested in stock. We can ship that today and you will get it in about two days. The rest we can produce in the next three days but shipping will be your challenge."

"Okay. Can you airfreight all your from inventory and the rest in three days?"

We can do it at our end Mr. Pilar but being a new customer on the first order, you will need to pay in advance."

Yeah right. Like I had a hundred thousand dollars limit on my credit card.

"Sure no problem," I said. "I'll arrange to get it wired to your bank as soon as they open tomorrow."

"Ah, Mr. Pilar, we can only ship once we have the money. I'm sure you understand," he countered.

"Grayson," I thought, you fucking Canadian capitalist asshole. "Of course, I understand. How about this? I will give you my credit card now for half and have the rest wired to you first thing tomorrow."

"Certainly, that can work," he said. "With the fees for the credit card added of course," he demanded.

What an asshole. I thought Canadians were supposed to be just nice Americans.

I gave him the details for my American Express card and after all the shipping details and wiring instructions were covered, I thanked him and hung up.

I called Ricardo to tell him the fuel problem was solved but I was going to need a little financial support and he laughed.

"You might say he has you over a barrel," he said laughing, "A hemp oil barrel that is."

"Fuck off, Ricardo," and he continued laughing even louder.

"I'll take care of it Finn, and by the way, the boat is looking good and my guys are impressed with its structure and set up. We should be competitive on race day."

"Just not too competitive, at least until we get Hank and Consuelo back," I reminded him.

Thinking of Hank I decided to call Matt. With the fuel problem solved I figured I could help him try to locate Hank and Consuelo.

I left a voice mail. "Matt, it's Finn. I wanted to let you know that things are looking good at our end. The boat is secure and we have a hemp fuel source lined up so I am available to help with the investigation. I have one idea I am going to work on but call me when you get this message."

As I hung up, Annalee walked into the room with a plate of sandwiches and a cold Stella. The sandwiches were Cuban mix with cheese, pork slices, ham and pickles plus mayo, lettuce, and mustard. They were cooked Panini style.

"Damn, girl, these look great." I almost added "And so does the waitress," but I realized that would only encourage her which would not be a good thing for my new monogamous self.

She smiled and did a little curtsy. "Can I be of any further," she paused, "service?"

Note to self - Behave.

I took a bite of the sandwich and gulped half the beer.

"Actually you can," I began. "When I first met Consuelo she seemed familiar. I don't think I ever met her before but something about her was ringing a bell. It might be the whole he/she thing and I guess I put it down to that and thought nothing about it, but now I'm not so sure."

"What's your question?" Annalee asked.

"Well, Hank said she was ex-Cuban Special Forces. She seemed to handle an M4 well in the firefight we had but . . ." my voice trailed off as I recalled the events.

"Does her accent sound Cuban to you?"

Annalee paused then said, "Actually no."

"What do you hear in her voice?"

After a moment she said, "Finn, you know that for many years Cuba was considered by the U.S. to be a Russian ally and we had thousands of Russians in the country as military advisors and technical experts of one kind or another."

"Yes," I replied not liking where this was going.

She is clearly fluent in Spanish but she speaks with a bit of a Russian accent."

"Oh, shit!" was all I could think of saying. This could not be happening. It was like somebody had just shot me in the gut.

CHAPTER TWENTY-ONE

"What?" she asked.

"Annalee, I think we need to get you back to Cuba and out of here as fast as we can."

"Finn, what is it? What did I say?"

"Look, I think this whole thing just got a lot darker and more complex that I could have imagined."

I put down the sandwich that had suddenly become an afterthought and called Hector. "Hey man, how far out are you from the house?"

"Stacy and I are about ten minutes away. What's up?"

"I need you here ASAP and get in touch with Matt if you can. We need him here now!" The urgency in my voice was clear and he replied, "We'll be there in seven."

Annalee was looking nervous. "What did I say?" she asked again.

"It's not you," I said trying to reassure her. "The Reader's Digest version of the story is that I have had several run-ins with the Russians in the past few years and generally speaking things have not gone well for them."

"When Matt and Hector get here I'll let you all know what this could mean for the case."

Hector as good as his word was back in seven minutes.

"Any luck getting in touch with Matt?" I asked.

"Nope, just went to voicemail."

"Okay, you need to know this so I will give you a quick recap. In the last few years, Matt and I have worked on a couple of cases that involved Russians. In Key West, Eastern Europeans run a number of businesses. A lot of the cosmetics and tee shirt stores are generally Russian-owned. Also, we were involved in one case that involved the death of a local guy whose father is a prominent figure here, a Bubba as we call them. He had a former Spetznaz mercenary as a body guard/hired gun, a guy named Vlad. As a result of some interesting events, Vlad went to jail for trying to kill us."

"Okay," said Hector, "What does all this have to do with *this* case?"

"Well, I have had a funny feeling about this for a while and had not been able to put my finger on the issue. Today I asked Annalee if she noticed anything odd about Consuelo who claimed to be an ex-Special Forces operator from Cuba. She said Consuelo's Spanish accent actually sounded Russian. There are a lot of Russians in Cuba because of their relationship with communist Russia. That's when the penny dropped." I paused for effect.

"She bears a striking resemblance to Vlad and no, not all Russians look alike."

"Fuck me," responded Hector.

"I'll pass but thanks for thinking of me."

"Are you saying," asked Stacy, "That Vlad or some family member is impersonating a transgender woman in order to take revenge for what, putting him in jail? And where does Hank fit into all of this?"

"I have no idea," I truthfully replied.

Hector asked, "How long have you known Hank? And how did you meet him?"

"I met him when I was working on the Key West Police force about five years ago. He was building a hemp-bodied sports car. I responded to a noise complaint and met him here. I liked the car design so I invested twenty thousand dollars for two percent of the company."

"So you've known him a while, but what about Consuelo?"

"Well, about three or four months ago his long time housekeeper and bodyguard just walked out on him so he hired Consuelo. He is always picking up strays and she seemed like just one more. I hadn't met her before a few days ago when we came here for dinner."

My cell rang and it was Matt. "Jesus man where have you been? We've been trying to reach you."

"I can't talk for long but what's so urgent?"

"We think we have found a Russian connection," I offered. "We suspect Consuelo is somehow linked to Vlad our buddy from the Cross case"

"Shit!" was all he said.

"Where are you?" I asked.

"I put a tracker on one of the SUVs from Blunt Force that I spotted watching Truman Waterfront by the boat. When they left, we followed them up to a trailer park on Cudjoe Key. I have my guys doing some recon and was going to call OJ."

"Call the Sherriff's Department. They cover that area. Do you think Hank and Consuelo are in there?"

"I'm just trying to figure that out. The SUV is parked opposite one trailer but they could have more on the property. We are checking for activity around them."

"Do you need help?" I offered. "Hector and his crew could be there in fifteen minutes."

"No, we're good. I'd rather the cops go in, as I don't want to get into a gunfight again. We've had enough of those in the last several days."

"Okay, don't be a stranger."

"Copy," was all he said.

I gave the group an update then we waited.

Thirty minutes went by then the phone rang. It was Matt sounding breathless. I put him on speaker.

"Well that was a waste of time," he began. "It looks like the trailer was a bunk house for the shift changes for the guys with Blunt Force. They were pissed that we interrupted their beauty sleep."

"Any sign of Hank or Consuelo?" I asked.

"No, but we did find a rental agreement for a big go-fast boat and it's not on site although there is a boat launch at the park. It may be the one they used to handle the exchange with Annalee."

"Where did they rent it from?" I asked.

"Already on it. Some place up on Key Largo. One of my guys is already following up but it's the first piece of hard evidence that may link Blunt Force to Annalee's kidnapping. If they are smart and so far they seem to be batting a thousand, it will be a shell company doing the renting but it's worth following up."

"See if they put trackers on their rental boats so they don't get misplaced," I said feeling frustrated. "Maybe we'll get lucky."

"Got it. Good thought. I'll get back to you as soon as we have anything," and he hung up.

I was beginning to fade and needed sleep. Being drugged and locked up in a storage locker for the night was not my idea of a good night's rest even though it was with Stacy.

Stacy must have read my mind because she came over and took my hand. "You need to get some . . . . ," she paused, "Rest," and she led me to bed.

I lay down and closed my eyes and in seconds was asleep.

I awoke with a start to the sound of chaos downstairs. Boots pounded up the stairs and the door burst open. It was Matt.

"Time to get up sleepy head."

"What time is it?" I asked.

"Time to go a-hunting."

I looked around and the sun was just coming up. I must have slept for at least ten hours.

"Coffee first?"

"On the road. Get dressed and we will head out," Matt commanded. He could get like that sometimes.

I looked down and realized I was naked. Stacy must have taken my clothes off while I slept and tucked me in. As I pulled on my jeans and a Green Parrot tee shirt I asked, "Where are we going?"

"To see an old friend I hope, up on No Name Key."

"I forget, how far is it to No Name?"

"I have no idea with the crazy traffic, but Google Maps shows it's about twenty-five miles from here."

As we headed out the door Stacy came up to me with coffee in a go cup. "Man cannot live on sex alone," she murmured with a smile.

The look of confusion on my face, as I assumed I had fallen asleep on her, must have been hilarious.

"Why sah, I do declare. You don't recall our most intimate and passionate evening. I am deeply, deeply hurt," doing her best Scarlett O'Hara impersonation.

Finally getting the joke I replied, "Frankly my dear, I don't give a damn."

She feigned shock then laughed. "Well, tomorrow is another day." With that, she tossed me a bag with a couple of toasted bagels and said, "Until then," with her head cocked to the side.

Matt drove and I rode shotgun. Two of Hector's guys were in the back.

As I wolfed down a bagel, I mumbled, "What's the plan?"

"Well, last night while you were catching about two hundred winks with the beautiful Stacy, some of us were working.

It turns out the rental company in Key Largo had a tracker on the go-fast boat. We were able to trace it to somewhere off the grid, a run down shack called *Slack off Mobile Marina.*

We thought it was worth a trip so we drove up earlier this morning. The boat is there and two of the SUVs that Blunt Force are using. They're next to an office/warehouse building. This may be their base, so I left a guy there to keep an eye on the place and came back for reinforcements."

"So what's the plan?" I asked again.

"Well with any luck we'll rescue Hank, and save the damsel assuming they're being held by Blunt Force."

"Okay, so what's the plan, for the third time?" I can be persistent like that sometimes.

"Basic building breach, high/low entry with flash bangs. Don't shoot unless shot at, you take the back of the building with one guy, I take the front with another."

He turned as he drove and said, "Lefty you go with Finn and Red you're with me."

"Copy that," they replied in concert.

We turned off U.S. 1 in Big Pine Key then drove over to State Rd 4a, passed No Name Pub, across Boogie Channel and parked the car on a dirt road a few hundred yards up onto No Name Key.

"We walk from here, " instructed Matt.

"Where is the guy you left here?" I asked.

"He's down by the water watching the building and the go-fast boat. It's over at the dock about fifty yards to the north of the building. He'll cover us if they try to get away using it."

"Has he seen any activity while he's been here?"

"None, which is a little odd but maybe they're late risers."

"All right listen up," said Matt. "Before we go in,

check comms, then weapons." We took a minute to make sure we were all on the same communication channel and all earpieces were working.

We then did a quick weapons check. I had taken a Glock from Hank's collection and checked it while we drove. Matt and the others had AR-15s modified to full auto plus they each had a Glock. I missed my old standby H&K USP .40 but it was back at my place on Catherine.

As we approached the building, I had a flashback remembering a village in Iraq while searching for Taliban fighters. It was not unusual for them to wire the building so when we breached it, it would blow.

The bagel felt like a hockey puck sitting in the pit of my stomach. The coffee was sour and churning as a bout of backwash brought it up in my throat. I'd forgotten the nerves before every breach.

Lefty and I headed around to the back of the building walking along the outside of a decayed wooden fence. When we were in position, I gave one click on radio.

Matt came on and calmly said, "On three. One, two, three."

Lefty kicked in the door and went in with his AR-15 held high and aimed left. I went in low aiming right. An explosion in the distance rocked the building.

"Motherfucker!" shouted Lefty as we glanced around. The building was still standing and we could see in the distance Matt and Red at the door in front. The building was empty.

Lefty and I raced through the building and out the front door. Debris from the go-fast boat was scattered and burning on what was left of the dock about twenty-five yards down the road.

CHAPTER TWENTY-TWO

Matt came over the radio, "Check-in. Everyone, okay?" There was no word from Matt's guy who had been on watch. Suddenly my phone rang.

"Finn, I hope you and your friends are okay," said a voice I recognized as the guy who had taken Stacy. He had not a trace of concern in his voice.

"Your man watching the boat should be okay as we set the explosion to radiate out into the water but one can never be sure as you would know considering your background."

"Fuck you, asshole," I said for want of anything more pithy to use as a rejoinder.

"Now, now, Finn, he chided. I would think you would be grateful it was only a warning and not intended to do harm," followed by a chuckle. The next time it could be more, perhaps targeted is the word I am looking for."

Suddenly a shot rang out and a window next to me that had not been damaged by the explosion developed a hole.

"Take care Finn," and he hung up before I could tell him he missed me.

"What the fuck was that? Take care?"

This guy has tried to shoot me, burn me, and blow me up. He's drugged and kidnapped me and kidnapped Stacy as a pawn to get the notebook. What's the pattern I'm missing?

Suddenly the light came on. They're not trying to kill me; they're keeping me busy and off guard but causing minimal actual harm. We've been dodging bullets and bombs but not really getting hurt. So far the girl was killed on the boat, one of the Blunt Force guys in the boatyard and one of Dale's guys with the RPG. *For all that is going on, you would think there should be a higher body count.*

I walked over to Matt who was in the process of dusting off his man who had been knocked down by the explosion of the go-fast boat.

"I think I'll give your guy a new name Matt. How about Dusty?" I laughed.

Dusty smiled weakly shaking his head to clear his ears. "It beats Boomer."

I appreciated his sense of humor.

"Matt, I just had a call from the guy who blew up the boat. I think it may have been 'Whiney' King."

"What did that fucker want?" demanded Matt, clearly pissed off.

"That's the thing," I replied. "He didn't seem to want anything. It's almost as if he is just playing with us, distracting us from something real."

"That fucker has killed one of Dale's guys, drugged you, kidnapped . . . . " I cut him off.

"Hang on, I'm just saying, for all the drama in the past few days, the body count is still low."

He paused.

"What are you saying?"

"I'm not sure. It's just for a while now, my 'Spidey sense' has been tingling. Something is off. This guy could have taken us or at least me out at any time, yet he hasn't. Why?"

196

"Okay, go on," encouraged Matt.

"How about he wants us to accomplish something? He keeps the pressure on so we are so busy running around that we don't look for what's *really* going on. Suppose what he wants is for us to race the boat and prove the fuel concept?" I conjectured.

"That's crazy. Why go to all the trouble? If that's the case, he could have just let Hank make the fuel and race *his* boat."

"Yeah you're right," I replied. "How about this then? Dupree Petroleum hires Blunt Force to steal the notebook and keep us running around with our dicks out while they try to figure out the formula but Hank has a missing piece."

"Then they figure out that they need Hank to complete the puzzle and kidnap him," Matt added.

"Exactly," I agreed. "But so far this is not different from our current operating assumption."

"Actually, we *are* learning something," I smiled. "They want us to lose the boat race which tells me that they don't want the fuel to be successful. I suspect that they want to bury the formula so they can continue to sell oil."

"You mean like steel, paper companies, and cotton producers lobbying against hemp for car bodies, paper or clothing. In fact, like Standard Oil did to Henry Ford in the 20s against ethanol?" *It's clearly not just me who has been on Google lately.*

"Precisely," I agreed. "But more than that, they accomplished two things by taking Hank. Leverage on us and the last piece of the formula puzzle."

"All right, so assuming your supposition is correct, what do we do now?" Matt asked.

"Look the piece that doesn't fit in this puzzle is the girl."

"The girl on the boat?"

"Yeah, of course, the girl on the boat dude, you

need some sleep. You're firing on only one cylinder."

He nodded and we headed to the car in hopes of avoiding the Sheriff's Department. Someone was sure to have called the explosion in by now.

As we walked back toward where we had parked, I puzzled, "The question is who did it and why kill her? Also, what happened to the rest of the crew?"

"Blunt Force did it," replied Matt. "Doesn't it seem obvious? Torture, then kill the crew to find the notebook. When they can't find it, kill the girl to keep her quiet and to send a message to Hank that they are serious."

"Yeah, almost too obvious," I began. "Look, Blunt Force has done a lot to minimize the damage to us and these guys are not assassins, they're soldiers."

My head was starting to ache and I wanted to get back to Stacy. It was starting to get hotter and the humidity was rising as the sun rose higher over the island. My bagel carbs from earlier were starting to wear off and I needed more coffee if I was going to recharge. Being shot at and bombed all first thing in the morning was a bit much. I needed a break.

We were driving off the island as two Sheriff's cars and a fire truck raced by us barely glancing at our SUV.

~ ~ ~

We got back to the house and after updating Stacy I told Matt I wanted to talk to Abacus and check on the boat.

"I want to talk to Abacus about anything else he might remember about the morning the boat rammed into his out on Wisteria. Also, I want to check on the preparations for the races. I'll be back in a couple of hours."

"All right son, but don't get into any trouble, eat your vegetables and no drinking," he chuckled.

"Yes mom," I replied coyly.

Stacy, Crutch and I hopped into the replacement Mustang Stacy had arranged while Matt and I were out getting shot at and bombed.

~ ~ ~

As we slowly drove toward Old Town, signs of clean up from Hurricane Margaret were starting to appear on the sides of the road. Piles of debris were organized along every street which made driving even more of a challenge on the already small roads. Appliances from flooded homes were out on the street ready for insurance claims. I'm amazed at how many old refrigerators, stoves, and stacked washer dryer sets get damaged by flooding but somehow newer ones rarely do.

You could hear the buzz of chainsaws mixed with the usual sound of waves and ocean breezes in the palm trees as we drove down South Roosevelt past Smathers Beach. The road was flooded with about three inches of salt water as we approached the turn by the 1800 Atlantic Boulevard condos. The north side of the road always has problems after a rain; this was just a little more than usual.

My thirst level was rising with the heat as I parked on Catherine Street in front of my house around the corner from the *Mockingbird*. Crutch seemed excited to be home but equally happy when instead we walked toward the *Bird*. We were a little ahead of the lunch crowd but Abacus was at the bar serving a couple of regulars.

"Hey, Finn!" he yelled out. "How're the STD treatments going?"

The regulars laughed, a couple of tourists at a table looked up, Stacy being used to it smiled indulgently and I shot back, "No worries Abacus, I'll cover your girlfriend's treatments but tell your mom she's on her own!"

We all laughed and I ordered Stacy a Chardonnay, a Bud Light for Crutch and a Stella for me. The three of us sat at the bar. It almost felt normal. *Almost.*

I asked Stacy to stay at the bar with Crutch and I went into the kitchen to talk to Abacus.

"Abacus, I'm working on a new angle on the girl on the boat and wanted to ask you a few more questions."

"Girl on the Boat. Was that the sequel to *Girl on the Train* and a prequel to *Girl on the Plane*? Sounds like the title of the old Dionne Warwick song."

I paused for a second. "Wow, you're obscure this morning."

"Just tired of the questions. First the Coast Guard, then the cops, then you, now you again. I've told you everything I can remember," he said putting emphasis on the *everything.*

"Just humor me for five minutes," I pleaded.

He stared blankly at me. "What do you want to know?"

"Take me through the morning starting before the boat rammed yours."

He began, "I was sitting in the salon of *Blue Agave* with a fresh cup of French press and my usual day old apple fritter from *Croissants de France* on Duval."

"Do me a favor and close your eyes to picture exactly what happened next."

He looked at me and as if indulging a small child, took a deep breath and sighed. "So I am three bites in on the fritter and am just taking my first sip of the coffee when BAM, the boat lurches forward on its anchor line and the coffee splashes all over my shirt and best shorts."

"Great, what did you hear?"

"You mean besides the grinding of fiberglass, the wrenching of bowsprit jamming into the wheel of my boat and my yelling 'What the fuck?' while the coffee scalded my balls?"

"Yes."

"My footsteps pounding up the ladder to the deck?"

"Okay, what did you see?"

"Jesus Finn, we've been over this already. It was a raggedy old boat jammed up the ass of my pretty little sloop like an old queen on a young lover."

"Needlessly graphic, but funny," I mused. "What else?"

"I yelled out for the captain, and got no response so I climbed aboard, opened the hatch and went down into the salon."

"Okay, go back a bit. Before you went down into the salon," I paused. "Close your eyes again and look around the boat. Picture it in as much detail as you can. Where were you moored? Other boats around you? Anything. It's important."

He paused and I could see the wheels turning. "Nothing." He paused. "No, wait. I did notice a girl climbing out of the water onto a small powerboat about thirty yards away."

"What did she look like?" I asked excitedly.

"Strangely I remember she had long dark hair but when she climbed out of the water onto the boat, she had on a small bikini."

"Yeah, and . . . ?"

"The odd thing was, she had a very muscular body. It didn't really register at the time but thinking back she was almost like one of those body builder types you see on the bottles of drugstore nutrition supplements. It was a disconnect but I wanted to go below to find the captain so I just forgot about it. Sorry."

"No problem dude. What did she look like?"

"I only saw her from the back so I didn't see her face but as I think about it, she sort of moved like a guy too." He paused and added, "I can't put my finger on it but you know guys move differently than women."

Can I have an amen for that?

"What happens next?"

"I opened the hatch and went below to find the captain but only found the girl. I came up and puked over the side from the stink then went back to my boat to call the Coast Guard."

"When you came up and puked, did you see the small boat with the girl on it?" I asked.

"No, she was gone by then."

"Could she have swum from your boat to hers in the time it took you to get on deck and then climb over to the other boat?"

He thought about it for a minute then asked, "Are you thinking she was on the *Kilimanjaro* and rammed my boat then jumped and swam away?"

"I don't know but it just seems strange that of all the boats in the moorings off Wisteria it slams into yours and kicks off this whole crazy mess."

"Well, fuck me," he said. "Why would somebody do that to me and who is this chick?

"I have no idea but we clearly need to find out."

~ ~ ~

I went back out to the bar and Crutch was entertaining the tourists with his doggy *Cirque de Puppy* routine. I tucked a buck in his collar and went to the bar to talk to Stacy. I gave her the update and she gave me a funny look.

"Finn, could somebody be trying to get to you through Hank and Abacus?"

"What do you mean?" I asked.

"I don't know. It's just strange. You know the cousin of the girl on the boat that rams into another boat owned by a guy who is your business partner. The boat she is on is transporting a notebook for your friend Hank who then calls you to help him with a problem." She paused, "You *do* seem to be the common denominator."

Damn, there's a reason I love this girl.

I paused. I just said that again. *Did I say it out loud? She was looking at me in a funny way.*

Just then Crutch came over and jumped up on his bar stool. He was wagging his tail as he stood on the stool with about ten one dollar bills tucked in his collar. Stacy and I both laughed at the same time. *Saved by the puppy.*

"Looks like you have a new revenue stream to add to your business," she said giggling.

~ ~ ~

I suggested we get lunch and continue this conversation with some food. We eat all the time at the *Bird* so I suggested the *Blue McCaw* on Petronia. They have a great Bloody Mary bar and we usually split the Baked Brie in a pastry shell with the fig and mustard preserve and a couple of fish tacos.

As we walked over from the *Bird*, we spotted an old friend of mine from Martin's. Harry Street was a Scotsman from Glasgow who came to the island twenty years ago as a photographer for National Geographic. He ended up making it his home when he was not traveling around the world and after retiring he settled here permanently. Harry is six foot five inches tall and somewhat of a legend in Key West.

We were surprised to see him walking a dog. He was wearing his usual cargo shorts and a tee shirt with a camera around his neck and a lens bag on his shoulder. As he got closer I could see that his new dog was a mutt with an Australian Sheepdog body and a pit bull face. The striking feature was that it had three legs with the back right one missing.

As we shook hands in greeting I asked, "New dog?"

Harry paused then smiled clearly loving his new friend. He knelt down and scratched her behind an ear and in his still thick Scottish brogue he said, "Aye, I got her about five months ago from the Humane Society. They rescued her after some asshole hit her then drove on leaving her by the side of the A1A. The vet had to take her leg off but she's a bonnie lass and has recovered nicely."

Crutch obviously agreed with him as he sniffed around her while she stood calmly on the sidewalk. He stopped and looked at her. He was clearly smitten.

"What's her name? I asked.

He grinned, "I call her, Tripod."

She looked up as Stacy and I burst out laughing. "I love it!" we both said at the same time.

We chatted amicably for a few minutes and I asked what he was up to these days.

"I'm headed down to Truman Waterfront to take pictures of the offshore racing boats and some of the teams for the Super Boat World Championships Magazine," he replied.

"Hey, that's great. Can we hire you to take some shots of our boat?" I asked.

"You've got a boat in the races?" he said somewhat astonished. "I didn't know you had the coin to play in that game."

"I don't, but a friend of mine has been at it for a long time. You might know him. Ricardo Ramos?"

"Aye, the tequila guy, right? Yeah, I'll be taking some shots of his new boat for promotional purposes. Heard it's an interesting boat," he added.

At this point, Crutch and Tripod were standing face-to-face like the two lovers in the Disney animated film, 'Lady and the Tramp'. All they needed was a bowl of spaghetti and they could have shot the remake.

"These two seem to have hit it off. Let's set up a play date at dog beach by Louie's," I suggested. "We can catch up over happy hour and these two can get more acquainted."

"Sounds like a plan. Let me know when you can make it."

We parted company and as we walked away, Crutch lingered pulling against his leash. I turned and for the first time noticed the back of Harry's tee shirt. In bold letters, it said *SERVICE OWNER*.

Stacy and I burst out laughing again and I said, "Good thing Christmas is coming."

At the Blue Macaw, we ordered our food then walked over to the Bloody Mary Bar. The first of its kind in Key West, it has two stations for creating a build-your-own Bloody Mary. With about a dozen different kinds of Bloody Mary mix, multiple salt mixes for the rim and hundreds of spicy sauces, you can create every imaginable Bloody Mary on the planet. You can top it off with your favorite garnish from the traditional lemon and celery or dill pickles to blue cheese olives, bacon, pearl onions, and pickled carrots.

Stacy and I each created our favorites and were enjoying our brief respite from the chaos of the last few days when our food arrived.

I was actually feeling as if my life, for a moment at least, was what I had pictured island life should be: a beautiful woman by my side, a great Bloody Mary in hand and a fish taco with Caribbean Jerk seasoning on my plate.

This girl had some kind of magic about her that was putting a spell on me. We sat for the next twenty minutes simply enjoying each other over the innocence of a simple meal. Crutch lay between us on the ground with his daily Bud Light half-finished, seemingly lost in contemplation.

After lunch, we continued to walk toward the Truman Waterfront along Whitehead then down Southard.

I remembered my relationship with Courtney my

ex-wife. She was the reason I was in Key West. Ours had been a fiery, passionate but tempestuous marriage filled with drama and intrigue that ended badly.

Stacy seemed to sense I was with her but not with her. "Everything okay?" she asked.

"Yeah all good," I replied after a pause. "Actually never better."

I reached over taking her around the waist and kissed her. It was one of those Hollywood kisses, slow and tentative at first then a full-on deep dive followed by tender and gentle. We came up for air and she said, "Take me now, big boy."

Actually, what she really said with a smile, "We need to go to the Blue Macaw more often."

After a moment she asked, "What's gotten into you?"

"I think after the last few days I've realized that you are in Tampa and I wish you would stay here. Crutch needs you."

Crutch looked up at me as if to say, "Yeah sure, throw me under the bus once again you coward."

She looked down at Crutch and said, "Yeah I've noticed he's developed quite a drinking problem and he needs some female companionship."

She looked back at me again and waited.

Damn women.

We walked a little further and she still waited.

"Stacy," I struggled. "Stacy."

"Finn," she said smiling gently.

I took the plunge. "Since we met, you have bewitched me, body and soul. I never wish to be parted from you from this day on." I took a deep breath.

Stacy leaned toward me and kissed me gently, "Jane Austin, very sweet, but you left a part out."

I swallowed. "I love, I love, I love you."

"And I you," was all she said. And she took my hand

as we walked along in silence.

The next few minutes were a blur. *Damn, I thought with a flash of panic, now I really have gone and done it.*

CHAPTER TWENTY-THREE

We continued our purposeful ramble to the waterfront and arrived as several barrels of fuel were being offloaded from a flatbed truck next to *our* catamaran. Ricardo looked up and seeing us waved us over.

"I am glad that you two are here in time! The fuel just arrived and we're next in line for a crane to lift us into the water," he said excitedly.

Our boat was on her side on the trailer waiting with five others to be lifted into the water in the harbor. Once fueled up, we could fire up the new engines and warm them up. Then we could take a couple of laps around the course, as it is the first shakedown to test all the different critical systems: rudders, props, throttles, telemetrics, gauges etc.

As I ran my hand over the hull, I was struck by the surface sheen and slick exterior. The mobile crane came alongside our trailer and the crew began placing the padded straps used to lift her off the trailer. Slowly the engine of the crane began to growl and the boat lifted up off the trailer. As I watched, the sponsor name on the lower pontoon came into view, *Tequila Mockingbird* in large script lettering.

I turned to Ricardo and he smiled, obviously proud of what he had done. "I like it, mi amigo." *Was that a tear in my eye?*

The first pontoon gently entered the water and as she began to float, the second was lowered as well. Once she was fully in the water for the first time, Ricardo stepped on board and with a bottle of his family's hundred percent Agave Tequila, he christened her by striking a metal cleat used to tie fenders.

As the bottle shattered he said, "I christen you the *Kilimanjaro Snow*. Long may you beat the crap out of these other boats!" Then he climbed into the driver's cockpit while the throttle man climbed in next to him.

Crewmembers began fueling the boat while others checked each of the compartments to look for any sign of leaks. Once fueled, the crew chief confirmed the radios and telemetries were operational then they fired the first engine.

One of the big twelve hundred and fifty horsepower Mercury racing engines roared to life and gently it was warmed up then set on a slow idle. All the gauges and radio signals were confirmed operational. The second engine was fired up and the check out procedures repeated.

Once both engines were operating at idle and all the steering and prop settings in place, the crew untied *Kilimanjaro Snow* from the pier and she began slowly making her way out of the harbor past the Danger and Fury fleets and into the Key West Channel where the race would take place.

In theory, this boat could hit speeds of two hundred plus miles per hour in calm water but until the engines were broken in over the next couple of days, Ricardo and his throttle man Eleazar would follow a careful plan. We were running new engines on a new fuel in a new boat.

Stacy and I watched for about thirty minutes as they ran the boat back and forth in the Key West channel each time going a little faster. They were testing prop settings, engine temperatures, fuel consumption, throttle responses, and a dozen other metrics in preparation for the first race.

As we stood watching, Harry came up to us and said, "Nice looking cat, dude." We again exchanged greetings as Crutch gave his undivided attention to Tripod who seemed interested but coolish.

We watched for another few minutes when my phone rang and it was Matt. I had almost forgotten the whole investigation for the afternoon and he brought me fully back to reality.

"Where the fuck are you, Finn?"

"I'm down at Truman Waterfront with Ricardo working on the boat." So I exaggerated a little. "What's up?"

"Have you forgotten we are still looking for Hank and Consuelo?" he asked.

"No actually I have some news," and I walked him through the information I got from Abacus and Stacy's theory about me being at least part of the focus of all this chaos.

"So what she's saying is someone is actually after *you* in this deal?"

"Well, yeah. We haven't put it together but what if someone wanted me to get involved in this investigation so they had some woman drive the Kilimanjaro into the back of Abacus' boat?"

"That doesn't make sense," he said, "Why would they do that?"

"I don't know but . . ." I paused. "What if the woman who Abacus saw swimming away after the collision was actually a man? Who . . . ."

Another pause, then Matt asked, "Could it have been Consuelo?"

For a moment I dismissed the idea but I thought

for a minute. Consuelo was supposed to be a Cuban Special Forces operator. She had only been with Hank for a few months but could have known about his plans to get the notebook back from Cuba and could have helped locate the boat to bring it back. Hank knew about the relationship *I didn't have* with Annalee.

Consuelo could have been the one to fire shots at the house and had the M4 to do it. But what about all the other stuff? The RPG at the Old Island Boatyard, drugging Stacy and I at the storage facility, kidnapping Stacy and blowing up the go-fast boat on No Name Key?

"Dude we're coming back there now. We need to talk," and I hung up calling Stacy over as she was chatting with Harry.

"Time to go." Crutch looked desperately disappointed but we walked back quickly to pick up the car. We needed to get back to the house and compare notes with Matt.

As we drove north, Stacy and I kicked around different ideas but it kept coming back to Consuelo plus maybe some other player or players. Consuelo knew what we were planning and what our forces were as we brought in Dale and Matt. She could have told someone outside the house we were going to the storage facility; hell she could have kidnapped Hank and shot Dale.

A lot of the pieces were still missing but an image was beginning to form. It felt like we had the general framework but needed more information. Much like putting together a jigsaw puzzle, we had at least most of the edge pieces in place but the main picture was still just a collection of several dozen parts of the puzzle and a bunch of orphan pieces.

We cleared Cow Key Bridge headed north on U.S. 1 and stopped at the light. The car behind seemed to have been caught by surprise and gently bumped into the back of our rental. The driver, an elderly woman, got out of her car to check for damage, as did Stacy and me.

The woman appeared to be in her seventies and seemed a bit shaken by the fender bender. I came around to the rear of our car as she was inspecting the damage when suddenly she pulled out a pistol from her purse with a suppressor attached to the end then pointing it discreetly at Stacy.

A deep male voice said, "I will shoot your girlfriend, if you don't climb back into the car slowly," then he fired a shot into the trunk of the car.

Hertz was really going to review my rental agreements in the future.

I climbed back into the driver's seat.

"Stacy, get into the other car. Spare keys are in the trunk. If you try to follow us I will shoot him." She shot the trunk again.

Grandma then climbed into the back seat of our Mustang and put on her seat belt while to me she said, "Don't put on your seatbelt."

So there went my Plan A which was: I buckle up, get up to speed then slam on the brakes or slam into a pole.

Keeping the gun pointed at my back, below eye level, she commanded, "Now drive, north."

I took off watching Stacy in the rear view mirror scrambling to get the trunk open to find the keys. I hoped she thought to call the Sheriff to report this before we turned off the highway.

As it happened, it would not matter as we turned off U.S. 1 near the CVS as soon as we were out of sight of Stacy. We drove about two hundred yards turning into a gated parking area. My elderly captor then pulled out a gate opener and once we were inside, she directed me to pull over next to a gray Ford Taurus.

"Get out, slowly," she muttered in my ear.

We each climbed out of the Mustang and she then tossed me the keys.

"Open the trunk," she demanded.

I complied still looking for some edge to gain the upper hand. As if reading my thoughts she fired a shot into the trunk near my hand as I opened it.

"Ventilation," she said coldly. "Now get in."

"Can we talk about this?" I asked in my best pitiful pleading voice.

She fired another shot. "The next one ventilates you."

I guessed she had been watching too many old James Cagney movies.

"You dirty rat," I said as I climbed into the trunk.

She slammed the trunk lid and a second later the engine started and we took off out the gate and I could tell that after a quick right, we were back on the highway headed up the Keys.

It seemed we drove for about thirty minutes but grandma had taken my phone and watch before the car switch. *I hated the idea of losing another phone.*

After several turns and onto progressively rougher roads, we turned onto a paved section then my accommodations suddenly got darker. The trunk opened and I stiffly climbed out. It appeared we were parked in a framed area beneath a house on stilts. Cheap plastic lattice panels covered three sides of the area and a tarp was dropped across the entrance after we had driven in making it impossible to see in or out.

"What have you done with grandma?" I asked the man standing four feet away from me with a pistol pointed at me.

"Pick up the zip-cuffs on the ground in front of you, take off your shoes and put the cuffs on your ankles," he demanded. This guy was good. I started to bend down to get them thinking I might be able to lunge under his gun to tackle him when he fired into the trunk again.

So I complied and once I was hobbled, he tossed a second pair of cuffs to me and demanded, "Put these on, behind your back."

Once hog-tied like a calf at a rodeo, I was basically screwed as a pair of hands shoved me from behind. I collapsed slamming my head onto the bumper of the car. Everything went black.

~ ~ ~

I came around to find myself with a canvas bag over my head and sitting on a hard wooden chair.

After about ten minutes, as I continued to play at being unconscious, a hard voice said, "Once a person regains consciousness, their breathing changes. You might as well quit trying to pretend. You've been awake for ten minutes."

I said nothing trying to determine my captor's accent and to listen for the sounds around me as well get hints of smells.

"I think you have the wrong guy, my friend," I began. "Nobody is going to pay for my release and I have nothing of value to offer you."

"Oh but Mr. Pilar, you do have something we value," he replied.

I felt the bag ripped off my head and I was staring at a face I somehow knew. An icy feeling crept into my bowels and it was all I could do to keep from pissing myself.

"I see you can see the family resemblance, Meeester Pilar."

The pieces fell into place. Without the makeup and wig, Consuelo bore a vague resemblance to the Russian Spetsnaz Special Operator I had disfigured then jailed during my last little adventure. Her/his unusual Spanish accent was gone and a hint of his Russian roots could be heard.

The slam of the pistol to the side of my head interrupted my reverie and after a minute clearing the ringing in my head, I responded, "Funny, but your brother Vlad never mentioned he had an ugly sister."

He laughed, not the reaction I had hoped for. "You Americans, always with the gender slurs." He hit me on the other side of my head. Ambidextrous I thought as I blacked out again.

I did my best when I next came around to manage my breathing. The bag was back on my head but I remembered the layout of the room. A window was on my right, a door on my left. I took stock. My naked body was on a wooden chair and there was a lump on each side of my head.

~ ~ ~

My new captor's brother Vlad was a mercenary working for the gay lover of my ex-wife's also gay husband. *It's complicated.*

I had killed my ex-wife's husband with a spear gun during an offshore fight when they were trying to kill me. Her husband's lover then tried to kill me and I was able to survive a fire in which Vlad and the lover were badly burned, then captured.

All this time I had been thinking this latest episode was about oil and hemp fuel formulas when it was really about revenge. Now at least half the puzzle was becoming clearer.

"Ah," said a new friend, as he came into the room, "It appears you are awake again."

The bag was again torn off my head and I looked up to see someone standing next to Vlad's brother. I was now truly terrified.

"Sorry, Finn," my friend said.

CHAPTER TWENTY-FOUR

Before me stood my old friend Hank looking a bit battered but very much not a captive.

" I suppose you have some questions."

"Ya think?" was all I could muster.

"You can probably guess that this doesn't end well for you," he began. "I'm sorry but I needed that notebook and my colleague here, his name is Viktor, was looking for some help from you so we teamed up so to speak."

Hank seemed a little nervous even with me tied up and naked.

"I'm sorry but tell me again how you two hooked up. I must have missed that memo. Was it the national convention of the Fraternal Order of Duplicitous Assholes?"

Viktor stepped up and hit me again but this time with his fist.

Hank stepped in again, "Finn I understand you're confused and upset. Let me back up a bit. About four months ago, Consuelo approached me about the housekeeper position I had advertised in the Key West Citizen. She spoke Spanish and was from Cuba so she seemed like a perfect solution to my problem. I needed someone to get the notebook in Varadero and to bring it back here. Her special forces background was perfect for me as I was concerned that Dupree Petroleum was looking for it as well."

"So where do I fit in with all this save the planet bullshit?"

"You Finn are a small but important piece. Viktor needed a contact in Cuba who we could trust because he couldn't go back because of some problem with a drug smuggling charge I think," he said looking at Viktor who nodded.

"I remembered during one of our conversations that you had met an attractive tour guide during your last trip to Cuba and that her parents lived in Holguin and ran a Casa Particular *Cat on the Moon*. I gave Viktor the name and he took care of arranging for the girl to get the notebook. It turned out he got this girl *Nieve* rather than the girl you knew, but whatever. I went over and worked with the charter captain to hide the notebook in the sailboat."

I began feeling sick at this point knowing that because of me Nieve was dead and most likely also Lon and Rosie, *Kilimanjaro's* captain and his first mate.

"Viktor, took care of the rest, dropping the captain and his first mate off on one of the deserted Bahamas islands then sailing back to Key West. We got you involved by ramming the sailboat *Kilimanjaro* into your partner's boat."

"I got the notebook; Viktor wanted you. It seemed like a fair trade to save the planet."

"I still don't get it, why did you need me? Just for Viktor?"

"My grandfather was very shrewd. The formula requires a special enzyme to break down the biofuel feedstock and produce the octane levels we need. The enzyme was identified in the notebook using a simple book cipher. As you probably know, a book cipher is a popular method for encoding messages. In my grandfather's case, the name of the enzyme was needed to accelerate the biofuel process. If you know the name of the book, you can decipher it. I already knew the book but needed the notebook to get the cipher. They can have the notebook because it is useless without knowing about the book title."

"Son of a bitch!" I exclaimed.

Hank continued, "I figured these guys would be chasing around after the notebook and the harder we tried to keep them from getting it, the more important they would think it was. In reality, it simply bought us time to test the formula. I didn't think they would actually kill to get it or I would have turned it over right away to them."

"So let me get this straight," I shouted angrily. "You used Nieve, got her killed and conned me all to keep these guys chasing their tails while you tested the formula?"

I was straining in the chair panting and screaming at him.

"Nieve is dead. Annalee was kidnapped. I have been beaten and shot at. I killed at least one person, then was arrested, twice, all so you can keep our mysterious friends busy so you could confirm your precious formula?"

He looked unmoved, then added, "Finn, you have to understand." He shouted like a mad scientist, "This formula can change the world! I knew these Dupree Petroleum guys would either use it for their own profit or bury it!"

"And," he continued, "So Viktor could get his revenge."

His eyes took on a weird glow like I imagine every

fanatic gets when they are in full wacko mode. The hint of madness was scary coming as it did from someone I had known for several years.

I turned away not knowing what to do next. How was I going to tell Annalee her cousin had died simply to buy time for Hank to test his fucking formula? What, so he could save the world?

But I guess I had to get out of this little predicament first.

Hank seemed to be winding down and I needed to buy some time. I figured Stacy would have gotten to Matt by now and told him about our suspicions about Consuelo. With any luck, Dale might have come to and would be able to point the finger at her as well. They would not know about Hank though. I needed to stay alive until they could put the pieces together.

"So Hank, I'm still a little confused." I decided asking for a little information might buy me some time. "How do you expect to get away with this little scheme? We already know about Consuelo. She was spotted swimming away from *Kilimanjaro* after you rammed Abacus' boat and Dale will know who shot him because he survived."

They looked at each other and Viktor shrugged and said, "By the time, we're done here and if they ever find your remains, I will be long gone. My flight leaves in the morning for parts unknown. But I know where *you* are going for destroying my brother's life."   With that, he took out his gun and pointed it, first at one leg then at the other, then at one shoulder then the other. "Ah, where to begin?"

I yelled, "Wait!" as he pulled the trigger.

I screamed as the bullet tore into my left calf shredding the muscle and shattering my shin. Pain like that is impossible to forget and I nearly fainted as I collapsed, tipping over the chair and hitting the floor.

Viktor grinned clearly enjoying my suffering.

"I am going to kill you!" I screamed, "If he doesn't first!"

Viktor paused with a look of confusion on his face. He turned to see Hank pointing a gun at him.

"Sorry Viktor, but you are the only person other than Finn who knows I have been involved at all in this. As far as the world is concerned, I'm an innocent kidnap victim."

Hank pulled the trigger and shot Viktor in the chest stopping his heart instantly. Viktor crumpled to the floor with a look of astonishment on his pale face.

Hank continued, "I will be the hero who after being kidnapped was able to escape his bonds. I have already taken care of the guy who brought you here. Unhappily, I arrived too late to save my old friend who had first been tortured then shot by Consuelo, the duplicitous housekeeper. She had kidnapped me and beaten me to get a secret formula for the evil Dupree Petroleum Company."

Hank walked over and picked up Viktor's fallen gun off the floor where Viktor dropped it.

He pointed it at me and said, "I'm sorry my friend, I truly am, but sacrifices are a part of every great cause and you are dying so millions will live in a world that doesn't need fossil fuel to power progress."

I looked at him and said, "Oh for fuck sakes, spare me your sanctimonious, tree hugging bullshit and shoot me you asshole."

I figured it was as good an exit line as any given my condition; besides my leg hurt like a bitch.

I kept my eyes open looking up at him, perhaps thinking he would not have the courage to pull the trigger. His eyes had a strange brittle look, dark and opaque like obsidian. He raised the gun pointing it at me then his head exploded before I even heard a shot.

His gun jerked and fired, the bullet hitting the floor an inch from my head. My bladder finally let go as his body hit the floor, the gun firing again. His finger spasms pulled the trigger again and again, with bullets flying through the air. The gun finally clicked empty as the last shot grazed my shoulder.

I must have fainted because my next memory was being wheeled on a gurney toward a waiting ambulance as morphine kicked in and I floated away on a cloud.

~ ~ ~

The next day or so was a blur, with faces floating in and out of my hospital room with looks of concern on the faces of some and relief on others. Slowly I began to focus and could stay awake for five to ten minutes at a time. I recognized Stacy, Matt and even OJ came by with Crutch, who licked my hand, farted and lay down at the foot of the bed. I need to reconsider his diet, I thought out of the blue as I drifted off again.

I guess the doctors began to lighten the morphine drip because I came around with the sun coming up and Stacy sleeping in a chair by the bed. I tried to sit up and grunted with the pain in my chest. She woke up.

"Easy big guy, you have a couple of extra holes in your body."

"Did they damage my good side?" I asked.

"Which side would that be?" she replied with a smile.

"The one without the scars from the time I was here last year," referencing the stab wound and gaff scar on my right side caused by my ex-wife.

"Well think of the new ones as adding symmetry." She grinned, "I'm a half-full kind of girl, as you know."

We chatted for a little about nothing then I asked the question I was stumped by, "So how the hell did you find me?"

Stacy smiled and said, "Crutch."

I must have looked confused then incredulous as the story unfolded over the next few minutes.

"When you got back in the car after we were stopped, Grandma got into the passenger side. Crutch had jumped out when I got out and stood by the side of the car."

"As you started to pull away, I was scrambling to find the keys to the car that Grandma said were in the trunk."

"I know," I added. "I was watching you in the mirror as we drove off."

"Crutch took off running after the Mustang while I searched the trunk. Once I found the keys, I got the car started and took off after you but you were out of sight. As I got to the CVS turn, Crutch was barking by the side of the road. I slowed to pick him up, but he took off running up the street and up to the gated parking lot. Our Mustang was parked in one of the spots and an old guy in a sweaty old Margaritaville tee shirt was putting a note on its windshield. I pulled up and asked if he saw who parked it."

"The same assholes that parked a gray Taurus in my parking spot," he cussed. "I've been watching the spot all afternoon to catch them in the act but I had to pee. When I came back they were just driving out so I called the cops to report it."

"Which way did they go?" I shouted back at him racing back to the car and sounding like an old west movie.

"They went that-a-way" he replied in character, pointing back toward the highway. It must have been the most excitement he'd had in a while.

I tore out of the lot and headed north figuring I was only a few minutes behind you.

I called OJ and within five minutes he had an APB out to the Sheriff's Department as far up as Marathon.

The old guy was sharp and had given the plate number when he reported the parking violation. After driving for about ten minutes, OJ called to say the car had been spotted turning onto a gravel road on Big Coppitt Key.

By the time I got there we had lost you but at least we had narrowed down your location. I waited by the highway on the gravel road to make sure Grandma didn't double back while Matt and OJ pulled together a search.

It took us about three hours to narrow things down to the house where we found you."

"All I ever saw was the lattice work walls of the garage. Where did they keep me?" I asked.

"They set up a room under the house beside the garage. We were able to see through the window that you were in the room. We were gearing up for an assault when we heard a shot and saw that Viktor was shooting at you then Hank shot Viktor. At first, we thought Hank had saved you, but when we saw him point a gun at you, Matt took him out."

"Where is Crutch now?" I asked. "I think he deserves a steak."

"I called Harry to see if he could take him while you were recovering so he could hang out with Tripod," she grinned. "I expect Crutch will see that as reward enough."

I laughed, "Good thinking."

I was beginning to fade again and realized I was not yet ready for prime time.

"How long have I been here?"

"Two days," Stacy replied.

"Damn, what about the races? Have they started? How are we doing?" I tried to get up but collapsed back on the bed.

At that moment Matt came into the room and answered my question. "Congratulations Finn, you are the proud sponsor of the second place finisher on the first day of the Super Boat International Offshore Racing Unlimited Class!" He pulled a bottle of Champagne from behind his back, unwrapped the foil and popped the cork.

A nurse came in tut-tutting and fussing about alcohol in the hospital but Matt ignoring her, poured several plastic glasses of Veuve Clicquot and we toasted our success.

After a brief celebration, it was obvious I was fading and the room emptied as I drifted off to sleep with Stacy by my side.

After another day in the hospital, I was able to twist Digger's arm to pull some strings and get me released. My leg was in a full cast and I would have eight weeks of recovery to allow the muscles and tendons to heal then probably six months of rehab learning to walk again.

In the interim, I wanted to at least watch day three of the offshore races so Matt and Stacy arranged to take me down by van to the Waterfront to watch our boat launch. Ricardo was supervising the launch as they lowered the forty-eight foot catamaran into the water.

For the first time, I noticed that a new name had been stenciled on the stern of the boat. 'Cat on the Moon' with the logo from the Casa Particular owned by Annalee's and Nieve's parents. It seemed the perfect way to honor Nieve. I only wished Annalee was there to see it but she had already gone back to Cuba with Nieve's remains while I was out of it in the hospital.

~ ~ ~

Ricardo and his throttle man Eleazar, climbed into the shared cockpit and after some adjustments, they fired up the first engine. A deep throaty roar echoed across the harbor and after a minute or so it settled into a level, reverberating rumble. They fired the second engine and it too settled into a matching synchronized growl. It almost sounded like the throaty roar of a pair of big lions preparing to pursue fresh prey on the African savanna. *I thought of Hemingway and had to smile.*

Ricardo began a couple of slow circuits around the racecourse to warm up the engines. Stacy loaded me quickly into the van then drove me over the rough parking area and into Fort Zachary Taylor State Park where the best viewing area for turn three was set up.

A voice came over the loudspeaker to announce that the Unlimited Class race was about to begin.

There were four boats at this point in the race: the storied former winners Miss Geico and Dupree Petroleum; then the new boats this year, WHM and Tequila Mockingbird. After two races, Dupree Petroleum was in the lead on points with Tequila Mockingbird running a close second.

It was clear that a new rivalry was developing between the two leading boats. Now, after the death of Hank, Ricardo and I seemed to have assumed the mantle of the environmental challenger to the old guard.

Suddenly the announcer shouted that the race had begun.

I am sure that if I could have stood up, I would have been screaming and jumping up and down as the *Bird* rounded turn three in the first of ten laps. She was half a boat length back and charging after Dupree.

At speeds of over two hundred miles per hour on a perfectly smooth, almost glassy harbor, the racing between Key West and Sunset Key on the first lap was incredible.

Then as chop from the wakes of the boats in the race began to appear, the boats were bouncing clear out of the water with only the props seeming to skip and then float in the air. Speeds dropped but the pontoons would still rise and fall, twisting and yawing from one side to the other and from front to back and every position in between.

On the next circuit, Tequila Mockingbird was in the lead by a length and on the third Dupree took it over. It was almost like there were only two boats in the race. The lead change five times by the last lap and as the two boats came into the last turn, Dupree seemed to cut the corner sending a huge wake into the Tequila Mockingbird and the stern of Dupree seemed to clip our bow. Over the handheld radio Ricardo had given me, I could hear him hailing the judges to file a protest against Dupree.

I sat in the wheelchair waiting with my casted leg extended in front of me as Stacy walked back to the van for a couple of beers. It would take a few minutes for the judges to settle the dispute.

The barrel of a pistol has a very distinctive feel when it is pressed against the back of your neck. Even in the heat of Key West, it sends a chill down your spine.

CHAPTER TWENTY-FIVE

"Mr. Pilar, you continue to be a problem for us and I am beginning to grow weary of your interference."

Now what? I ran through all the already arrested or deceased players in this little drama. *Shit.*

I decided to take a shot and said, "Whiner, what the fuck do you want now?" Then I waited.

"The anger in his voice was apparent when he said, "It's Mr. Whiner to you, asshole."

"Mr. Asshole, if you don't mind, now that we have the introductions over with, I repeat, what the fuck do you want now?"

"All right asshole, here's the real deal," he snarled. "My employer wants the book used to decipher the code."

I decided to play dumb. "What book code, you already got the notebook. Can't all your smart guys at Dupree figure it out?"

The shot he fired beside my ear almost deafened me even coming from a suppressed gun.

"The next one will take a chunk out of your ear, now where is the book?"

What am I? A pin cushion?

I was tempted to say, "Could you please repeat that? I'm now deaf in one ear," but I didn't relish losing my hearing so instead I offered, "You guys are really dumb. I mean really dumb. Hank left a trail a mile wide so in the event that something happened to him, the world would still get his grandfather's formula."

"What do you mean?" asked Whiner.

"Look, somewhere along the line, Hank's devotion to green energy and sustainability turned from obsession to fanaticism. He knew the value of his grandfather's formula was that it could accelerate the process for producing biofuel."

The Blunt Force CEO made no comment so I continued, "His paranoia with Dupree Petroleum lead him to extreme means to protect the process, yet he was concerned that you might just kill him and the formula would be lost to the world. He selected a boat named *Kilimanjaro* to transport the notebook. It was I believe a coincidence that the girl they used as a dupe was named *Nieve*."

"I'm not following you," whined Whiner.

"*Nieve* in Spanish means *snow* you dumbass," I taunted. "You can tell your employer that they can't stop the formula from getting out to the world. The code you need is in *The Snows of Kilimanjaro*, Hemingway's famous short story. Hank left a trail of clues that a tenth grade English student could figure out."

Suddenly a new voice sounded behind me.

"Asshole, the gun I'm holding twelve inches from your head is an H&K USP 40. I am told that it would blow a rather sizable hole in your brain. You now have three choices."

I laughed as Stacy calmly said, "Door number one, you can shoot Finn and you will die as well."

Not my first choice I must admit.

"Door number two," she continued. "You can try to turn around and you will die or door number three, you drop your gun and dive off this pier. If you can't swim you will die but knowing you are a former Navy SEAL I expect door number three is your best option although frankly not my preferred one."

"Now choose, asshole," she said in the most amazing throaty growl.

I could feel the tension as his pistol dug a little deeper into my neck.

"I said, NOW. Choose!" Stacy repeated.

The pressure on my neck eased and his gun hit the pavement.

"Now hit the water before I change my mind and blow your head off anyway" she commanded.

Whiner dove into the ocean and swam for his life.

Stacy then leaned over and with a shaky hand passed me a beer.

I swung the wheelchair around and she jumped back to avoid my extended leg from hitting her. "I've told you before to be careful with that thing," she chuckled in an attempt to relieve the tension.

"Which thing might that be?" I quipped looking down at my lap. Despite the last few minutes, Stacy's complete command of the situation had me ready to go.

At that moment, a voice came over the PA to announce the winner of the Unlimited Class Race.

"After reviewing the race video, it is the ruling of the judges that Dupree Petroleum," there was a pause, "That Dupree Petroleum violated the rule regarding contact between competitors on the course. We are calling the winner of the race and the Super Boat Unlimited Class World Championship, Tequila Mockingbird!"

Over the radio, I could hear Ricardo and his crew

cheering.

Stacy sat on my lap. "I've never taken advantage of a man in a wheelchair before."

I kissed her and offered, "Let me give you a lift."

And that was the end of the beginning of that.

ϕ   ϕ   ϕ

National Bestseller

National Bestseller

The Next Finn Pilar Key West Mystery

I was almost three miles out and preparing to enter the landing pattern for Key West International Airport when the Cessna 172 engine sputtered once, coughed then died.

"Oh shit!" ran through my head followed by, "I'm fucked".

My mental curses seemed to fill the now silent but for the wind noise cockpit.

I paused and pictured my instructor walking me through the steps for an emergency power-off landing. There was nothing quite like a total engine failure on approach during your first solo flight to focus the mind, unless it was engine failure right after takeoff. My mind went blank until I realized if I didn't do something, my blank mind could become a permanent condition.

A quick glance at the altimeter told me I was approaching a thousand feet and dropping fast. The fuel gauge read a quarter tank so it wasn't fuel.

I could hear myself saying, "Trade altitude for airspeed. Maintain airspeed to maintain control. Distance is dependent on altitude, glide speed and descent rate. Ideal glide speed for the 172 is 68 knots"

Shit, I was never very good at math. I cursed my buddy Emerson, the owner of the plane for the absence of 'Foreflight' software that calculates all this stuff using GPS. Mine was sitting pointlessly on my desk at home. I could see the runway in the distance but couldn't see how I was going to make it.

Think faster idiot. Off my right wing tip now, about nine hundred feet down was South Roosevelt, four lanes of pavement running along the south shore of Key West between the airport and the beach.

Make a decision dude I thought. I needed to make the turn but that would peal off airspeed and accelerate my loss of altitude. I tried a restart. No Joy

"Mayday, mayday, mayday, Key West Tower, this is Cessna November seven, niner, niner, two. downwind for runway nine. I have total engine failure on approach to Key West"

"Cessna, November seven, seven, two, you are cleared to land nine?" came a tinny voice on my new Bose headset.

"Unable, altitude eight hundred feet."

I could picture air traffic control hitting an emergency switch to scramble the fire equipment and wave off other traffic.

"What is your intention Cessna nine, nine, two?" came the calm voice in my ear. My intention is not to crash and die, I thought

I made my decision, put on full flaps to maintain lift and began my turn to the right toward the now closer pavement.

"I will attempt to land on South Roosevelt," I responded and began to look for traffic in the northbound lanes. I could see Atlantic Boulevard now below me.

The first hurdle was clearing the antennas on the top of 1800 Atlantic Blvd. It was going to be close.

The road ahead was not a straight line but curved first left then right. The crowded beach would be on my right. A water landing was not an option with a rock pier jutting out from the beach and a row of tourists on screaming jet skis racing just off shore.

My speed had dropped to fifty-five knots and was right on the edge of maintaining lift. I was too low to clear the antennas.

I decided a hard landing was better than crashing into the building so I pulled back on the stick as I came toward the antennas and held my breath. I heard a bang and felt a bump as the fixed landing gear grazed the top of a satellite dish. That would throw off their HBO, I thought; sure hope they're not in the middle of a Game of Thrones binge.

At this point, Crutch who had been occupying the right hand seat realized something was wrong and dove under my seat. If he'd had a parachute he would have jumped. "You wanted to come on this flight" I said.

It may have been a welcome gust of wind the helped me clear the building but now I was no more than sixty feet off the ground, barely in the air and just clear of the power lines stretched across the road. *Damn I'd forgotten about those.*

Ahead of me, I could see that a scooter had just driven passed a burrito food truck parked on the side of the road and I would kill him if I didn't clear him. *Things didn't look good for either of us.*

I nudged the left rudder to drop speed and shifted to the center of the road and the double yellow lines. The traffic visible in the distance could at least see me coming and hopefully avoid a head on crash. I was also trying to avoid trashing my buddy Emerson's new plane, not to mention killing somebody, not the least of whom was myself.

Emerson, or RW to many, was a local author who had just published his fourth novel. It was a national bestseller climbing the New York Times bestseller list to Number One after only three weeks. Set in Key West, *Dirty Martini* was looking to be a real hit, but I digress.

At this point, my ride was dropping like a rock with about as much lift as a patio paver. The road came rushing up as I tried to maintain as much forward momentum as I could, while avoiding the scooter that flashed by me on my right as I passed him about ten feet off the ground. He swerved as the silent aircraft swept past. I couldn't resist a quick salute then I slammed the plane down on the road still traveling about forty knots. The undercarriage collapsed and the now grounded fuselage scraped along with sparks and asphalt flying behind me.

What was left of the plane skidded first left, then right, heading toward a concrete wall that ran along the beach. It slammed into the wall after one wing was torn off by a now horizontal Vendor Parking Only sign. "Not my best parking job." I thought as fuel from the wing tank poured onto the ground and my head slammed into the side window knocking me out.

Thank you for reading.
Please review this book. Reviews help others find
Absolutely Amazing eBooks and inspire us to keep
providing these marvelous tales.

If you would like to be put on our email list to receive
updates on new releases, contests, and promotions,
please go to AbsolutelyAmazingEbooks.com and sign
up.

Acknowledgements

Writing a book may appear to those who have not done it to be a solitary effort. The reality is it takes a dedicated team of editors, experts, and readers to produce the finished product.

First and foremost I would like to thank my wife Susan for her incredible job transforming my stream of consciousness writing style into the finished product you are reading. An accomplished writer herself, she devoted hundreds of hours, laughing at my weird story lines, providing candid feedback, correcting continuity issues and putting it all into the form of a readable book.

She transformed my drafts into what I hope you feel is an exciting adventure. We have been learning together and she deserves credit as much as this writer for the final product.

I would also like to thank several friends for taking the time to read and identify story discrepancies, editing needs, and grammar questions. Bruce Dietzen, Doug Bennett, Gil Herman, Richard Aniol and Paul Wasserman read the drafts providing expertise in a variety of areas including biofuel, hemp based products, and flying segments.

Finally, I would like to thank my publishers, Shirrel Rhoades and Chuck Newman at Absolutely Amazing E-Books for taking a chance on a new writer and publishing my first book, *Square Grouper* two years ago.

About the Author

Lewis C. Haskell is a former international corporate executive and today is a fresh water conch who has owned property in Key West for 15 years. A diver, sailor, and Harley owner, he can be found riding his bicycle around town most mornings or with a glass of wine at Grand Vin in the evening.

ABSOLUTELY AMAZING eBOOKS

AbsolutelyAmazingEbooks.com
or AA-eBooks.com

Made in the USA
Columbia, SC
25 April 2018